In this new book, *Are You Marriage Material?*, Pastor Kevin Adams has produced a practical, biblically solid manual that will help you create a sure foundation for marriage. He provides the wisdom right now that your younger self will thank you for later! This is one investment that will pay handsome dividends as you invest these truths in your life.

Bishop Dale C. Bronner, DMin
Founder/Senior Pastor
Atlanta, Georgia

Bishop Kevin Adams has masterfully penned one of the most profound and practical books on relationships. *Are You Marriage Material?* gives readers an in-depth look at the qualifications necessary for a healthy marriage. It challenges readers to live up to the same standard of expectation we project upon others. This is a must-read for anyone serious about getting marriage right.

Bishop Joseph Warren Walker, III
Senior Pastor,
Mount Zion Baptist Church
Nashville, Tennessee
Presiding Bishop,
Full Gospel Baptist Church Fellowship International

I0593903

Are You Marriage Material?

Are You
Marriage
Material?

The Key to Finding
The Right **Spouse**

KEVIN L. ADAMS

Marriage Material (Kevin Adams)
© 2019 by Heritage Publishing Nashville Tennessee

Published in Nashville, Tennessee, by Heritage Publishing

Library of Congress Cataloging-in-Publishing 2017942270

ISBN   978-0997431889

CONTENTS

FOREWORD

It is incredible how we can live in dangerous approximation to something, and even find ourselves totally immersed in it, and never know what makes it work or fall apart.

Most of our lives, we have extolled and even made deity the virtues of love as the substratum of a solid marriage. We have written exotic poems, composed romantic songs, created ageless plays, and idolized lovers of antiquity and modernity. So we seek solace and relationship tranquility solely on how we feel about each other.

We have concluded in our quest for a solid marriage that it is only on how much we love each other! Enough love will bring happiness and solidarity with a lifelong partner. The conundrum is how with this intense love and sexual enjoyment and fantasy, one out of every two marriages end in divorce, not to mention relationships involving people who are married but apart.

Kevin's God-given intellect tells us why and jolts us ebulliently from fantasy into reality. The shock is, the love of a dog can be no greater than the dog itself, and the love of a cat can be no greater than the cat itself. My analogous expression may seem crude or even obscene, but this book is on the road to convince us that the love from a lazy person is lazy love, the love from a disrespectful person is disrespectful love, the love from an evil person is evil love, and love from an irresponsible person is irresponsible love.

It stands to reason that the opposite is true. Love from an industrious person is industrious. Love from a respectful person is respectful. Love from a good person is good. Love from a responsible person is responsible.

Kevin has eloquently expostulated the Scriptures to teach in this book that love can be no greater than the character of the person who loves. Thus respect is fueled by the character's ability to handle responsibility and not solely by a feeling. You can be loved but not respected, and the fabric of that marriage will unravel.

Bishop, thank you for guiding us to the ultimate combination of responsibility, love, and therefore our ultimate respect: "For God so loved the world, He gave His only begotten Son that whosoever believeth on Him should not perish but have everlasting life."

God's love is equal to His responsible character, and that combination orchestrated a marriage that can never end.

What a book! Read it.

INTRODUCTION

As a pastor, I talk with many people who want to get married. However, I find that they haven't adequately prepared themselves for marriage. So after they get married, I'm counseling with them again. That's when they tell me about all the problems they're having, problems that could have been avoided if they had worked at becoming better marriage material *before* they got married.

If you're considering getting married, start now to become the best marriage material you can be. This preparation is a process that shouldn't be skipped or rushed; and for children of God, it should be undertaken with much prayer and guidance. If you're already married but feel that your marriage needs help, you can delve into God's Word with me and learn how to revive, refresh, and restore your relationship.

When God created Adam, He didn't immediately create a wife for him. Instead, God gave Adam several tasks to complete. Once Adam developed a relationship with his Creator and completed the assignments he'd been given, only then did God create Eve and present her to Adam. Then God gave them an assignment that they could only achieve together: "Be fruitful, and multiply, and replenish the earth, and subdue it: and have dominion over the fish of the sea, and over the fowl of the air, and over every living thing that moveth upon the earth" (Genesis 1:28).

In this book, we'll delve into the key areas of responsibility, promise, security, faithfulness, vision, submission, trust, honesty, ministry, and love. In each of these areas, we'll look at what God says and explore how He models these characteristics for us. In reading God's Word, you will discover biblically based methods that will help you prepare to be marriage material before you get married or to strengthen your relationship with your spouse. I'll even share personal stories from my marriage and show you how you can learn from my experiences.

Too many people are looking to celebrities, social media relationship goals, and the fantasy world of television and movies to shape and form their relationships. But I encourage believers to start with the Bible to find encouragement, support, and models for how God wants us to live in relationship with others, especially in marriage. Biblical couples weren't perfect; but in God's Word, we can find the answers to our most challenging relationship issues and questions.

Being marriage material takes work and preparation, but it's well worth it. With God's help, you can present your best self to your spouse and have a fruitful, successful relationship.

— Chapter 1 —

Responsibility

"And God blessed them, and God said unto them, Be fruitful, and multiply, and replenish the earth, and subdue it: and have dominion over the fish of the sea, and over the fowl of the air, and over every living thing that moveth upon the earth." Genesis 1:28

Most people approach marriage knowing that it will require a certain amount of responsibility, but learning how to shoulder that responsibility doesn't start with saying "I do." Learning how to take on responsibility usually begins at home and then continues at school, as parents teach their children to do chores around the house and teachers give assignments for students to complete. Once we are hired, we graduate from entry-level jobs to positions with titles, more benefits, and more pay, but we are also expected to work longer hours and to produce more.

When we enter into relationship with Jesus Christ, He calls us to be responsible for work in the Kingdom. As we mature spiritually, He expects us to move from "need of milk" to being able to digest "strong meat" (Hebrews 5:12). The Lord nurtures us as "children, then heirs; heirs of God, and joint-heirs with Christ" (Romans 8:7); and with each phase, we take on more responsibilities in the Kingdom.

A responsible person is one who is trustworthy, reliable, and dependable. He or she doesn't mind being account- able to someone else to carry out an assignment. In pre- paring to be good marriage material, or to improve within your marriage, learning to be responsible is key to relation- ship success. Each person in a relationship must assume some level of responsibility for the dynamic to work, but working together as a team also helps a couple shoulder the responsibilities to keep their marriage balanced and happy.

BEFORE GOD brought together Adam and Eve, the first couple, He gave Adam several jobs to do. First, God "put [Adam] into the garden of Eden to dress it and to keep it" (Genesis 2:15). Next, "God formed every beast of the field, and every fowl of the air; and brought them unto Adam to see what he would call them: and whatsoever Adam called every living creature, that was the name thereof" (Genesis 2:19).

These were no small jobs! The Creator God made Adam responsible for taking care of his first home and the garden. Then God charged Adam with naming every creature that He created. Only after Adam completed these tasks successfully did God then take "one of [Adam's] ribs . . . made he a woman, and brought her unto the man" (Genesis 2:21-22).

Once God brought Adam and Eve together, He then gave them responsibilities that they could only carry out successfully together: "Be fruitful, and multiply, and replenish the earth, and subdue it: and have dominion over the fish of the sea, and over the fowl of the air, and over every living thing that moveth upon the earth" (Genesis 1:28). In that command, God was calling the couple to be responsible to Him, to His purpose, and to each other.

AS WITH Adam, God has called you to do some things before you are joined with a spouse. Taking care of responsibilities now will better prepare you to do so after you get married. So before you head down the aisle, reflect on what you're responsible for right now and honestly determine whether you're successfully handling those responsibilities or if you need to improve.

For example, ask yourself, *Do I have a good relationship with God? Do I pray regularly? Do I pay tithes and give as I should? Is God pleased with the way I'm living my life? Do I get to work on time? Once there, do I work, or do I spend most of my time on social media? Do I pay my bills on time? Who can depend on me? Am I reliable? Am I trustworthy?*

If you're married, think about what God has called you to do within your marriage. Have you been obedient to God's Word as it relates to marriage? Are you committed to your spouse? Are you a responsible head of household? Do you create a positive environment at home or a negative one?

If your answers to these questions are negative, you have work to do. And the first step is to find out what the Bible says about responsibility.

ONCE YOU'VE learned to be responsible to God, your employer, and other people, then it's easier to imagine being responsible to a spouse and a family. But what are you expected to do once you get married?

The apostle Paul is clear in his directives to husbands and wives: "Wives, submit yourselves unto your own husbands, as unto the Lord. . . . Husbands, love your wives, even as Christ also loved the church, and gave himself for it" (Ephesians 5:22, 25). Spouses may argue over who will do the cooking, who will take the kids to school, or who will pay the bills. While those are all necessary responsibilities in the life of a married couple, the Bible isn't specific about who does specific chores.

What the Bible does say is that the husband and the wife are to give themselves to each other in love. Neither person is let off the hook and must shoulder his or her share of responsibility to make the marriage work.

Another responsibility in marriage is encouraging your spouse to grow into his or her best self. Some people grow discouraged in marriage and accuse their spouses of not being the same as when they met. "You're not the same person you were when we first got married!" they say. What they're really saying is that their spouses are worse now than they were before they got married. But whose fault is that?

The psalmist wrote, "Thy wife shall be as a fruitful vine by the sides of thine house" (Psalm 128:3). In other words, your spouse should flourish, blossom, and grow on your watch, not shrivel up and languish for lack of love and care. It's your responsibility as a husband or a wife to love and encourage your spouse. As with a tender plant that needs to be watered, nurtured, potted, and given just the right amount of light, a relationship has similar needs. A marriage that is neglected is one that won't last.

But a marriage that is tended, nurtured, and cared for will prosper. Husbands and wives should be growing closer together and sharing more intimacy as they stay together, and your spouse should be better off now than when you first married. But if your spouse isn't growing and flourishing more now, reflect on why that may be happening.

Are you carrying out your responsibilities to your spouse's spiritual, emotional, physical, financial, and social needs? Are you providing the proper environment for him or her to be a "fruitful vine"? Or have you left your spouse to wither on the vine because you're too self-centered, you're tired, or you've grown bored?

For some people, being married is more than they want to take on. They are overwhelmed by being responsible for more than just their own needs and wants. But they often marry anyway, caught up in the physical and sexual attraction, assuring themselves that if things don't work out, they will get divorced and move on.

But Jesus taught that God's intention is for a man and a woman to come together as one in marriage and not be "put asunder" and that divorce is not to be used as a "get out of jail free" card when a couple grows tired of each other. Jesus' disciples were taken aback by His teachings and wondered why anyone would bother getting married.

But Jesus assured them that some people "cannot receive this saying, [except] . . . to whom it is given." He went on to say that some people stay single for that very reason. Others stay single because they are called to Kingdom work, which makes being married impossible (Matthew 19:3-12).

So before getting married, it's important to understand the responsibilities you will be taking on. Most people would like to be married, if not now, then one day. But many of them aren't ready to shoulder all of the responsibilities that marriage requires. If you have adequately prepared yourself for marriage, then you can feel confident in moving forward. If you are not prepared, perhaps you need more time, or maybe you've discovered that marriage is not your calling.

WHEN YOU see that your spouse isn't thriving, it's your job to encourage and exhort him or her so your relationship can be successful. Even when things appear hopeless, sometimes you have to "[call] those things which be not as though they were" (Romans 4:17). A spouse can speak and make you feel ten feet tall and able to conquer the world or make you feel as small as a pea.

My wife saw things in me that I didn't see in myself; and if it hadn't been for her, I wouldn't be where I am today. As our ministry began to grow, she told me that she could see me preaching the gospel on national television and ministering at churches all over the country, but I didn't take her seriously. At the time, our church was in a small building that might have seated 300 people. But she encouraged me to look for a bigger building. I thought it would be a waste of time, but I decided to humor her.

First, we visited a banquet hall. To me, it was the perfect size. If we used this place, we could seat 700 people! But my wife wasn't happy, which made me angry. I couldn't imagine why she wouldn't be thrilled to have a place where we could seat more than double the congregation we had now. But she insisted that the banquet hall wasn't the place. I asked her where she wanted to go.

"Let's go to Memorial Auditorium," she said.

Was she crazy? That place could seat close to 5,000 people! But we went. As soon as we arrived, she said, "I feel God in this place!"

"And you, me, and Jesus are gonna be the only ones here!" I said, growing impatient with her grand dreams.

I tried to convince her that the place was just too big, but she told me, "No, the place isn't too big. Your vision is too small. If you trust God, in a few months, we'll be putting out extra chairs."

I was angry, but again I went ahead with it just to show my wife how wrong she was.

After three months of meeting at Memorial Auditorium, we had to put out extra chairs. My wife was right. My vision was too small.

My wife's responsibility was to help me see what had not yet happened and to speak life into my ministry. But for it to bear fruit, she had to keep nudging me, keep encouraging me, keep watering that word she had spoken because I would have given up and settled for the banquet hall.

MY WIFE and I are a team, and we've discovered that it takes teamwork to make our marriage successful. Galatians 6:2 says, "Bear one another's burdens, and so fulfill the law of Christ." Successful marriages are built on each person taking responsibility in the relationship, which fosters a spirit of teamwork.

If you're thinking about getting married, remember that you are going to be joining a team of two. Also keep in mind that you are on the same team, not opposing teams,[1] so when you make decisions about who's responsible for what in your marriage, decide based on how you and your spouse can feel honored.[2]

Responsibility should be shared, not fall on only one person and become overwhelming or suffocating. Keep in mind the individual gifts and talents of you and your spouse to help you negotiate what you can do best and what will be the most effective and efficient division of labor for your marriage.[3]

No doubt you've heard the saying "Teamwork makes the dream work." It's become somewhat of a cliché, but in essence, it's true. If your team is fractured and dysfunctional, you won't win many victories.

Think about a professional football team. There is a maximum of 53 men on each team. As individuals, each man is different. They come from different walks of life. They attended different schools before making it to the pros, they have different perspectives, and they have different personalities. Some are married; some aren't. Some have children; some don't.

But when they walk onto that football field, they play as one man. They are unified in their goal of winning and being the best athletes they can be. So if the quarterback throws the winning touchdown or the defensive tackle knocks down a pass, every member of that team benefits. If that team wins the game, every man on that team is a winner. By the same token, if the running back fumbles the ball, resulting in his team losing, then every man on that team lost the game—not just the running back.

In marriage, husbands and wives become one. They are individuals and have different viewpoints or come from different walks of life, but when they are united in holy matrimony, they become one team. When one spouse wins, the couple wins. When one spouse loses, the couple loses. That's why couples are encouraged to seek mutual cooperation for the strength, support, and well-being of their relationships. We can see that all the way back in Genesis.[4]

In the beginning, Adam and Eve lived in harmony in the garden of Eden. They worked and lived together, communing with their Creator God. But once the serpent deceived Eve, then fractures began to appear in their relationship. Eve blamed the serpent, and Adam blamed Eve. When God handed out His punishment, He didn't just punish the serpent or Eve. He punished and cursed them all and then cast Adam and Eve out of the garden.

God gave Adam and Eve certain instructions and responsibilities. But when they allowed the serpent to deceive them, as a team, they lost. They missed out on living in the paradise God created for them.

There's no escaping that with marriage comes great responsibilities. But you can ensure that you and your spouse are successful when you approach those responsibilities as a team and include God in your planning.

IF YOU need help preparing yourself to be more responsible, consider the following:

Examine yourself. Look at how you handle responsibility right now. Look for ways to improve. If you're single, you might find it helpful to talk with trusted friends, family members, or coworkers for encouragement. If you're married, talk with your spouse to determine how he or she feels about your current level of responsibility. You might also talk with your pastor or a marriage counselor for more advice.

Be committed. Sometimes the thought of all the responsibility that marriage entails is overwhelming. But marriage is a marathon, not a sprint, so you have to be prepared to be committed for the long haul. Commit to being responsible in your relationships, even if you have to start small. Commit to small tasks, and then take on responsibility as you go.

Speak life. When life gets rough, it's easy to lash out at your spouse and speak negatively. But that's not helpful or constructive. When Jesus addressed the seven churches of Asia, He had many complaints against most of them. But instead of starting out with what they were doing wrong, first, He addressed what they were doing right (Revelation

2–3). The Lord praised the churches' work ethic, their generosity, their love, or their adherence to doctrine. Only after He had given them positive feedback did He then address their shortcomings.

In marriage, it should work the same way. If you want your spouse to flourish and grow, it's your responsibility to make sure he or she knows what's going well, what's right about your relationship. Is your wife a good cook? Then tell her. Does your husband make sure your car is gassed up and clean? Thank him. If your wife is great at making sure the bills are paid on time, let her know how much you appreciate that. When your husband does the laundry every week, make sure he knows you are grateful.

Right now, think of at least three positive things you can say to your spouse. You don't have to say them all at once, but find opportunities to praise your spouse for what is going well in your marriage. Then when you have negative things to discuss, your spouse will probably be more receptive because you've celebrated him or her for all the positive things and you've created an environment of love and nurture that can withstand constructive criticism.

Reflect

Ask yourself the following questions. Answer as honestly and thoughtfully as you can. Reflect on your answers, and use them to help you prepare for marital responsibilities or to improve how you will handle them from now on.

1. What am I responsible for right now? Am I successfully handling these responsibilities (church, work, finances, self-care, other family obligations), or do I need to improve?

2. What responsibilities will I face when I get married? What does the Bible say are my responsibilities to my future spouse? (If you're already married, ask) What responsibilities do I face in my marriage? How am I living out what the Bible says about marital responsibilities?

3. When I reflect on marital responsibilities, do I feel overwhelmed when I think about taking them on, or do I feel adequately prepared? Is marriage my calling?

4. What can I do to improve how I currently handle responsibilities?

5. When I get married, how will I work to make sure my spouse becomes his or her best self? (If you're married, ask) Has my spouse become his or her best self since we married? If not, how can I help my spouse to flourish and grow on my watch?

– Chapter 2 –

Promise

"[Abraham] staggered not at the promise of God through unbelief; but was strong in faith, giving glory to God; and being fully persuaded that, what [God] had promised, he was able also to perform." Romans 4:20-21

When you plant the seed of a tree, all you have is a promise that one day that tree will grow and bear fruit. But before you get fruit, you've got to go through a process. The process begins with planting, which is hard, dirty, and time-consuming work. You've got to dig deep into the earth, plant the seed, water it, and then wait.

When you first begin a relationship, all you have is a promise of its fruitfulness. Many people go into relationships looking for fruit right away, and they grow impatient when there doesn't seem to be anything coming from all of their hard work. But God has deposited everything in those seeds that you will need to become fruitful. You just have to be willing to trust God through the process.

Romans 4:20-21 says that Abraham didn't stagger at God's promises because he believed that whatever God promised, He would perform. Being marriage material involves you believing that God has given you what you need to be successful and then developing the potential, the promise, that God has created in you.

TO BE good marriage material, you have to align yourself with God's promises. Once you understand exactly what God has spoken to you as it relates to relationships, then you're not willing to settle for anything less than the promise. If what comes your way doesn't look like God's promise, let it pass you by. That's because God is preparing you for what He has already ordained for your life from the beginning of time. So to be properly prepared, your whole life will need to be in accordance with that promise.

In Matthew 16:19, Jesus says, "Whatsoever thou shalt bind on earth shall be bound in heaven: and whatsoever thou shalt loose on earth shall be loosed in heaven." God's promise to you has already been decreed, declared, and purposed in heaven, and your challenge is to agree on earth with what God has decreed in heaven.

If you're struggling believing God's promises, first, remember that God cannot lie (Numbers 23:19; Titus 1:2; Hebrews 6:18). Unlike human beings, God can be trusted to honor whatever promises He makes. They come to pass.

Second, always align yourself with God's Word. The promises in God's Word serve to reinforce and strengthen weak faith. Reading how God came through for men and women in the Bible, despite their flaws and issues, will encourage you to hold on to what God has spoken over your own life.

Third, don't give up on God's promises. They are yea and amen (2 Corinthians 1:20). Perhaps you're over 40, and you're not married. Don't be discouraged. Consider this: How difficult is it to walk outside right now and find a rock lying on the ground? Probably not too hard. But how difficult would it be for you to walk outside right now and find a diamond just lying around? You'd probably say that that would be a lot more difficult. Of course, it would be. But why?

Because rocks are pretty common, but diamonds are rare. Also, to find a diamond, you'd have to take the time to dig for it, and you've got to be patient to do that. Proverbs 31:10 says, "[A virtuous woman's] price is far above rubies." So the more valuable something is, the more time it takes to find it and develop it. So instead of giving up on God's promises, think of yourself as a diamond who has yet to be discovered.

God's promises are not unprecedented. Search the Scriptures, and you will see where God made several covenants (Noahic, Mosaic, Abrahamic, and Davidic covenants). The Bible shows us that God makes bilateral agreements, or covenants between Himself and another person (or a group of people), which means both parties have responsibilities to uphold the agreement (Deuteronomy 28). God also makes unilateral covenants where He alone is responsible for upholding the covenant to another party (Genesis 15).

So when you are contemplating marriage, you don't just have the promise of finding the right person, but you can be confident that you're not going into your marriage with just you and your spouse. God promised that what He joins together, no man can put asunder. The pressure of getting it right is not just on you and your spouse, but God comes into the marriage alongside you and undergirds it with His power.

That belief and confidence in God should start at the beginning of the relationship so it can sustain it, because you will probably go through times when you no longer want to be in that relationship. But you will need to remember to stay in it because of God's promises.

God takes His promises so seriously that Ecclesiastes 5:4 says, "When thou vowest a vow unto God, defer not to pay it; for he hast no pleasure in fools; pay that which thou hast vowed." God makes promises and keeps them, and He expects us to do the same. In fact, it would be better never to make a promise than to make it and then break it.

As a pastor, I try to help couples understand this concept. In fact, during the wedding ceremony, as they are repeating their vows, I also ask, "Do you also make this promise to our Lord and Savior, Jesus Christ?" The reason I do this is so that they will understand that they're not just saying their vows, making their promises, to each other; but they're also making these promises to God, and He takes them seriously.

And in later years, if these couples find themselves going through marriage counseling and talking about divorce, accusing each other of not holding up their end of the marriage, the first question I ask is, "What did God do wrong?" I watch as they struggle to reconcile my question with their reality. I remind them that they didn't just make vows to each other. They also made vows to God.

At that point, they have to admit that despite what their spouses may have done wrong, God has done nothing wrong. I start with that and help them remember that God is trustworthy and faithful, even when they're not.

ABRAHAM AND Sarah's story is full of promise. In fact, from the time Abraham obeyed God's direction to leave Ur until the birth of their son Isaac, God's promise was all they had to go on. But to receive the promise, Abraham and Sarah had to navigate through unbelief, delay, and disobedience.

In Genesis 16, we see that despite what God had told Abraham about bearing a son, Sarah had grown tired of waiting. Like many of us, she decided to take matters into her own hands and "help" God fulfill His promise. When she was unable to have children after many years, she told Abraham (then called Abram), "The LORD hath restrained me from bearing: I pray thee, go in unto my maid; it may be that I may obtain children by her. And Abram hearkened to the voice of Sarai" (Genesis16:2).

It's understandable that Sarah (then called Sarai) would grow impatient for a child. In ancient times, children were considered part of one's wealth and legacy for future generations, so a barren woman often lived in shame because of her inability to bear children.

And Sarah's plan was perfectly acceptable in her culture when a woman was barren. Her husband could father children with her servants, and the wife could then claim them as her own. That way, not only would she rid herself of the shame of being barren, but she could also provide her family a legacy of children, even if they were born of her servants. But though this was an acceptable practice at that time, it wasn't God's plan for Abraham and Sarah.

Sarah fell into the same trap many of us fall into. We allow our emotions to blind us to what God has promised. We don't see anything happening, so we grow impatient and give up or try to make it happen on our own terms. But the prophet Jeremiah warns us against letting our emotions be our guide: "The heart is deceitful above all things, and desperately wicked: who can know it?" (Jeremiah 17:9).

God is not calling us to rely on our own hearts to guide us. Instead, like the psalmist said, He wants to order our steps (Psalms 37:23; 119:133); and He wants us to trust Him that in His timing, He will bring all things to pass (Psalm 37:5). But in her impatience, Sarah didn't just cause problems for herself and her husband, she also caused problems for her maid, Hagar, and Hagar's son, Ishmael, and for the generations to come.

Even once the promised son, Isaac, was born, Abraham and Sarah's test wasn't over. Could they still believe God for His promise? In Genesis 22, God told Abraham to take Isaac to the top of Mount Moriah and offer him as a sacrifice. But how could this be? How could God's promise come to pass if Abraham obeyed God and killed the promise?

But Abraham rose early in the morning, saddled his donkey, and took his son with him as they made their way up the mountain. He told Isaac that they were going to worship. Once they arrived at the place of sacrifice, Abraham prepared the altar, put the wood in place, and laid his son upon it. But just as he was about to plunge the knife into Isaac's heart, God told him to do his son no harm.

Abraham's experience is important for us because it shows that there are times when we have to sanctify ourselves before the Lord; and in the process, we have to be willing to put it all on the altar. There are singles who are believing God for marriage or couples who are reevaluating their marriages who need to be willing to put it all before the Lord and allow Him to choose what we keep and what we get rid of, to allow Him to cleanse us of our disobedience and unbelief.

The blessings of marriage don't come simply because you stand before a preacher and get married. They come because of the consecration and sanctification you go through to let God know that it's all His and under His control. While that should happen, ideally, before you get married, you can also go through the process within your marriage. What you'll find is that when you put it all before the Lord, He might not have to kill it after all. Just as with Abraham, who built the altar, gathered the wood, and provided the sacrifice, when you give God something to work with, He now has something to bless.

Paul talks about this in Romans 12:1-2: "I beseech ye therefore, brethren, by the mercies of God, that ye present your bodies a living sacrifice, holy, acceptable unto God, which is your reasonable service. And be not conformed to this world: but be ye transformed by the renewing of your mind, that ye may prove what is that good, and acceptable, and perfect will of God." We are to be a perpetual sacrifice to God so that we may be purified, sanctified, and consecrated for His use. When we avail ourselves in such a way, we then can be transformed and renewed and realize God's promises to us.

Being human, we are flawed; and there are some things we have to let die in us. But in being a perpetual sacrifice, we die to, or sacrifice, our own ideologies and place ourselves in position for Christ to resurrect in us His ideologies.

Abraham told Isaac that they were going to go worship on the mountain and then return. But in reality, the only way Isaac could have returned was if God had resurrected him. And God can resurrect whatever needs to be brought back to life.

Many times, God's promise for marriage can't live because of all of the ideological baggage we bring to our relationships. Often, that's what kills our marriages and delays God's promises. So all of our baggage has to die. We have to take it up the mountain and lay it on the altar of sacrifice and sanctify it before God.

LIKE A lot of people, when I was single, I had all these thoughts about how marriage was going to be. All my friends told me my life was going to be over once I said "I do," and marriage was going to be a ball and chain, so I was determined not to let any woman run over me.

I also didn't grow up with a father, so I was struggling to figure out how I could be what I had never seen. There would be expectations on me that had never been modeled for me before, so I wasn't sure how I was going to shoulder those responsibilities. Then God told me, "Watch how I am with my bride, the church."

But I made the mistake of trying to make my wife become like my mother. I told my wife how my mother cooked and how she ironed my shirts. My wife told me, "Then you need to go back home to your mother!"

I had to allow all of that baggage to die in me before God's promise could be resurrected. After reading Ephesians 5, most people think that women have the hardest job submitting to their husbands. But I disagree. Paul tells husbands that they have to love their wives as Christ loved the church. Christ died for the church! So husbands have to climb up on their own crosses and die. They have to die to every woman in their past and to all their ideologies of what they think marriage should be.

For example, I used to tell my wife that in order to be a first lady of the church, she would have to wear fancy hats on Sunday and sit on the second row. Well, my wife had braids, so she wasn't interested in wearing hats, and she refused to sit on the second row. She and God needed me to let all that die so something else could be resurrected, and I'm glad my wife is who she is today instead of who I was trying to make her be.

If you're struggling with receiving God's promises to you regarding marriage, perhaps you're hanging on to emotional baggage that needs to die. Look at what you're carrying. Examine your heart. If there's anything that isn't in line with God's Word, lay it before the Lord, and let Him take it away.

A DEAR friend said that God gave him a vision to build a $15-million-dollar church, with a large television ministry to go with it. But just as his church completed the project and got ready to move into their new building, my friend was diagnosed with stomach cancer.

When I found out, I was devastated, and I was struggling to find words to encourage him. But he told me not to worry. He said that God hadn't changed His mind about what He had promised. I was confused. He said, "I've still got the promise. God wouldn't let me build all this if He was going to let cancer take me out."

It's the same in our relationships. Like Abraham and Sarah, we go through difficulties; but we can't allow our circumstances to make us doubt. God's promises haven't been overruled because you run into trouble or because you are disobedient. Sometimes your circumstances will look completely contradictory to what God promised, but you have to trust Him instead of what you see.

Years ago, my wife and I were going through rough times. I would leave the house angry. Then I would return home and immediately start an argument with her. I did that because it made me feel better about my own inadequacies and insecurities, especially when she argued back. I felt justified. I would say, "See, that's the reason I left!"

One night, I came home, ready for the argument to start. But when I got there, she was praying. I couldn't believe it! Even worse, she was praying out loud so I could hear everything she was saying. She was telling God all kinds of things about me. I said, "Don't talk to God about me!"

But as I heard my wife pouring her heart out to God, I was condemned. I promised her that I would be a better husband, which I thought would appease her, but I'll never forget what she said next.

"Didn't you hear my prayer? I'm praying that you'll be a better son to God, because if your relationship with God is right, I can live off the crumbs of your commitment to Him. So I'm not praying that you do right just by me. I'm praying that you get right with God, because if you're not right with Him, you won't treat the kids right. You won't treat me right."

I couldn't pick fights with her anymore because all she would do is pray, and that humbled me. I came to a point where I knew I had to do right, because if I didn't, my wife was going to tell God.

That experience taught me that we can either be a brick wall or a mirror to our spouses. If we are a brick wall, they can never see themselves for who they are. But if we are a mirror, our spouses can see who they are and what they're doing. Many times, it's that glance in the mirror that reflects back to them how they should be walking in God's promises.

IF YOU struggle believing God's promises, consider the following:

Hold on to God's promises. When you only have a promise from God, you've got to hold on to it, no matter the cost. Hold on to it, even while you're going through pain and you're enduring the process. Remember, when the enemy attacks you, he's not fighting you alone. He's fighting God's promise to you. He's hoping that he can fill your heart with discouragement and doubt so that you'll give up or, as Sarah did, try to fix your situation on your own, therefore messing it up and detouring from God's promise. When you start walking in doubt, then you don't believe and trust God, so you live outside of His will.

Fortify your belief in God's promises through His Word. God's Word is filled with promises made and promises kept, and reading it will reinforce and sustain your faith. Search the Scriptures to see how God came through for His people and those who believed in and trusted Him. Then pray God's Word back to Him, even when your faith is small. In so doing, ask God to help you trust Him and His timing as you watch God fulfill His promises in your life.

Develop patience and endurance. Pray for a measure of faith to believe God, no matter what your situation looks like, especially when you're going through delays and denials. When a seed is planted, that's not the end. There are days of waiting, watering, pruning, and weeding before the fruit comes. Don't invest all that labor just to give up before the promise is manifested in your life. Just as you're about to give up, the bud is about to appear and then blossom. If you've walked away from it, you've just prepared it for someone else to come along and enjoy. Be determined that no one else is going to eat the fruit of your tree.

Watch the company you keep. Watch who you allow to speak into your life (Psalm 1:1). Everyone is not equipped to handle what God has promised you. Surround yourself with people who pray, people who believe God, people who speak positively. Beware of those who give plenty of advice but don't have any evidence of it working in their own lives.

Reflect

Ask yourself the following questions. Answer as honestly and thoughtfully as you can. Reflect on your answers, and use them to help you to trust God's promises, no matter what your circumstances look like.

1. What promises have I already seen fulfilled in my life, for example, healing, salvation, miracles, blessings, deliverance? (Make a list of those promises fulfilled, and refer to it when your faith in God's promises grows weak.)

2. What are God's current promises to me?

3. What makes it difficult for me to believe God's promises?

4. How does the example of Abraham and Sarah's story speak to me as it relates to God's promises?

5. What strategies can I employ to better hold on to God's promises?

– Chapter 3 –

Security

"He that dwelleth in the secret place of the most High shall abide under the shadow of the Almighty. I will say of the LORD, He is my refuge and my fortress: my God; in him will I trust. . . . He shall cover thee with his feathers, and under his wings shalt thou trust: his truth shall be thy shield and buckler." Psalm 91:1-2, 4

We live in a broken and sinful world, and it seems nothing is secure. Our neighborhoods, schools, workplaces, and even our churches come under threat from those who would do us harm. But most people want to live, work, play, and worship free from danger. If there's one place we ought to feel protected and safe, it is in the presence of those we entrust our hearts to, our spouses.

That's why Jesus said, "What therefore God hath joined together, let not man put asunder" (Mark 10:9). If we can't rely on anything else, we should be able to trust what God has joined together. But, unfortunately, some marriages aren't as secure as they should be. Couples aren't enjoying the pleasures of married life because, deep down, they don't completely trust each other. They don't feel secure in their relationship.

Perhaps they're beginning to see cracks and fissures in a once-stable relationship. Maybe they've noticed their spouses are distracted and spending far too much time away from home. Whatever the case, couples must talk with each other (talk with a marriage counselor, if necessary), figure out what's going on, and begin to mend their faltering marriage. As with faulty plumbing or wiring in a house, insecurity isn't a problem that can be ignored in a relationship. The sooner couples address the problems, the better it will be for their future together.

Security is vital to any successful marriage, and husbands and wives should work to make their relationships as safe and secure as they can be. Many times, that involves establishing boundaries that keep negative influences and negative people out of their marriages; but it also means working with each other to provide security within the relationship.

FROM THE beginning, God had security in mind when He put Adam to sleep and took one of his ribs. The ribcage is part of the body's skeleton that surrounds and protects the internal organs. It's amazing that God would remove one of the ribs, meant to keep Adam's internal organs safe, to create Adam's bride, a woman who would need safety and security. Adam's ultimate responsibility to Eve would be to protect her, provide for her, and be her priest and prophet.

When Adam came together with Eve, Adam said, "This is now bone of my bone, and flesh of my flesh" (Genesis 2:23). In other words, he was saying that he and Eve were connected, and to take care of her was to take care of himself.

Adam and Eve's first ministry assignment was to care for the garden of Eden, the home God had created for them. But taking care of the garden also meant protecting it from detrimental forces, anything that would enter that would be harmful.

Our relationships are the same way. It's our responsibility to keep our relationships secure. We're not supposed to allow anything detrimental or distracting to enter our relationships with God or with our spouses. As with Adam and Eve, though, the serpent entered and distracted them from their purpose, and mankind is in the shape it's in today because of that security breach.

God first gave Adam instructions about the tree, but Adam failed to keep Eve secure from the serpent. His silence in the face of the serpent's lies and Eve's disobedience created an environment of insecurity for Eve because Adam wasn't reminding her of God's word.

When Jesus was crucified, He was pierced in the side, the same place Eve was taken from Adam. But Christ protects and keeps His bride, the church, and speaks His word over her. What began in the garden brought insecurity for mankind, but Jesus spoke from the cross and said it's finished. He reestablished security for all the church.

THE MOSAIC law made provisions for the security of family members who needed help. The Law instructed the closest male relative to deliver or rescue family members who were "in trouble, danger, or [needed] . . . vindication."[1] This male relative was known as a "kinsman-redeemer."

In the Book of Ruth, we see a kinsman-redeemer take on the responsibility of keeping Ruth and her family safe. Because of the death of her husband, Elimelech, and her sons, Mahlon and Chilion, Naomi had decided to return to Bethlehem, the city she and her family had left years before because of famine. But now, she had two daughters-in-law who were making the journey with her. Naomi discouraged them because she had no more sons for them to marry; and as a widow, she knew she couldn't provide any type of security for them. One of her daughters-in law, Orpah, turned back; but the other, Ruth, resolutely decided to stay with Naomi.

The two women arrived in Bethlehem at the time of the barley harvest, and Ruth went to work right away, gleaning in the fields. She happened upon Boaz's field. When she told Naomi of Boaz's kindness to her, Naomi knew just what to do. She knew Boaz, "a kinsman of her husband's, a mighty man of wealth" (Ruth 2:1), and she instructed Ruth to put herself in position to get even closer to Boaz. Ruth obeyed her mother-in-law "and did according to all that [Naomi] bade her" (Ruth 3:6).

That night, Ruth found Boaz asleep, and she lay at his feet. When he discovered her there, she asked that he cover her with his cloak. The next morning, Boaz protected Ruth from what could have been an incident of shame and scandal. He covered her with a veil, so no one would know who she was. And he supplied her with grain so that it would not appear that anything scandalous had happened during the night. Boaz was protecting Ruth physically, but he was also protecting her emotionally and protecting her reputation.

In Psalm 91:4, the psalmist talks of God spreading His wings over us. He also said, "He that dwelleth in the secret place of the most High shall abide under the shadow of the Almighty" (Psalm 91:1). The psalmist is illustrating for us an image of God's security, covering, and protection.

Boaz woke up in the middle of the night, and Ruth was in a vulnerable place at his feet. Anything could have happened to her. Other men were all around, and anyone who saw her there would have gossiped about her motive for being with Boaz. But Boaz, being the godly man that he was, told Ruth he would protect her.

WHEN ORPAH turned back, she was acknowledging that she wasn't in it for the long haul. But Ruth made it clear that she was going to stay with Naomi, no matter what. There are people in our lives who are there only temporarily. They're like scaffolds. Scaffolding is a temporary tool that builders use to help them to get a building up. But when the building is finally up, the scaffolding comes down.

Some people marry spouses who are like scaffolding. We try to keep them for the long term, but they're not built for that. They were never meant to be long-term partners, and they can never give you the security you need.

Ruth said to Naomi, "Wither thou goest, I will go; and where thou lodgest, I will lodge: thy people shall be my people, and thy God my God: Where thou diest, will I die, there will I be buried" (Ruth 1:16-17). In other words, Ruth was telling Naomi not to worry or feel insecure because Ruth was committed to their future and was going to be with her unconditionally.

Most people look at Ruth as a love story, and it is; but they miss the business deal that transpires in the story. While Boaz was a near kinsman to Naomi, he wasn't her closest one. Boaz promised to protect Ruth, but he made her aware that there was another man who was closer to Naomi than he was. He kept his word and contacted the man who would have been first in line to marry Ruth, but the man wasn't willing to do so. He had the right to marry her and the money to take care of her, but he didn't want the responsibility.

Insecurity happens when a person is not committed and is not willing to go with you all the way along your journey. An insecure person will get what they can out of you and move on, but they won't commit to you long-term. The closer kinsman knew he would have to buy Naomi's land, take care of it, and take care of any children Ruth had—all in the name of Ruth's dead husband. And for him, that was not a win-win situation, so he didn't see the value in marrying Ruth. It probably seemed like too much trouble.

Everyone's not equipped to handle what you bring to the table. They can't accommodate what it would take to be with you, so they pass you by. But God knows what you need, and He knows they wouldn't provide the security and protection He wants you to have. So He provides a Boaz who will step up and take on whatever responsibility there is in order to keep you safe and secure, no matter what it takes.

Boaz would redeem the property, redeem her dead husband's name, and redeem their children. So Ruth went from gleaning, gathering the leftovers of the harvest, to being the wife of the owner of the field!

THERE'S A deacon in my church who has had a long-lasting impact on my life. He worked two jobs, one of which was any side job he could get his hands on. He would cut grass and fix lawn mowers, stoves, irons, and anything that needed fixing.

One day, I asked him, "Why do you work so hard?"

He pointed to his wife. "You see that woman over there?"

At 70 years old, his wife was strikingly beautiful.

He said, "When she looks good, I look good. Son, don't ever forget that the woman is the glory of the man.

When that woman drives up, I never want a man to have to look on her hand to see if she's married. When she steps out of her car, and the men see Armor-All on the tires and the car waxed, they'll know there's a man somewhere. Now if your woman pulls up in a dust bucket, those men will wonder. So make her feel secure by providing the security she needs."

And so I patterned myself after his wise words. I almost went broke trying to keep up with him, but I do it anyway.

NO MATTER how rough it gets, don't become your situation. In reality, Naomi should have probably been the one to marry Boaz, since he was her nearest kinsman, not Ruth's. And Naomi was probably still young enough to marry and have children because the Bible mentions that she was able to nurse babies (Ruth 4:16).

But after losing her husband and sons, Naomi had become bitter, so much so that she told people not to call her Naomi but to call her Mara, which means "bitter." Instead of finding joy in returning to her home in Bethlehem, she talked about how much she had lost in Moab and that she had grown old. She had been through so much hurt and damage that she felt empty. She allowed her situation to break her.

Ruth, too, had lost a husband and the means to have children. But unlike Naomi, she didn't become her situation. When God provided the security she needed, she was open and ready to receive Boaz. She didn't allow her wounds to keep her from God's purpose for her life.

It's hard to provide security in a relationship when you're still harboring unforgiveness, bitterness, pain, grudges, and insecurity from your past. No one is safe with you. Maybe you didn't have a father who was there for you. Maybe an ex treated you badly. Maybe recently you've lost more than you've gained.

Once you've built up walls of protection around yourself, it's difficult for you to see God or to provide a safe place for your spouse. You don't have a clear revelation of God because you're so focused on your own pain. But once you purify your heart, forgive, and let things go from the past, you can see God and the person you're with, who is now able to see God in you.

Unfortunately, Naomi brought all her negative baggage with her to Bethlehem and became as broken as her past. But Ruth left all her pain and hurt behind in Moab. And when God was ready to rescue her from her poverty by sending Boaz, Ruth could be open and vulnerable enough to receive him.

If you're struggling with issues of security in relationships, consider the following:

Prepare yourself to be a Boaz. Being able to provide security for someone else takes preparation. When Ruth appeared, Boaz didn't have time to get ready. He needed to already be ready.

If you're going to keep someone else secure, you've got to be ready to do what it takes. So examine the spiritual, emotional, financial, physical, and professional aspects of your life. How prepared are you to provide for someone else? Are you in right relationship with God? Have you let go of past issues that may be keeping you behind walls of unforgiveness, bitterness, anger, and hurt?

How are your finances? Are you physically up to the challenges of providing for someone else? Are you faithful and honest at work? If you're single, use this time before you get married to adequately prepare yourself to provide the protection and security your spouse will need. If you're married, reevaluate your situation. Are you protecting your spouse and keeping him or her secure? If not, how can you do a better job?

Prepare yourself to be a Ruth. Ruth didn't just show up in Bethlehem expecting someone to take care of her. She went to work in the fields right away to glean the leftovers from the harvest. She didn't turn her nose up at her menial, low-level job, either. She worked to the best of her ability and made a good impression on the boss, Boaz. Then she listened to her mother-in-law, Naomi, and did as she advised to prepare herself for Boaz. In doing that, Ruth had to make herself vulnerable and put herself in a precarious position; but she was obedient, and it paid off.

Zone in on what makes you secure. Figure out what true security is, and look for that in a potential spouse. Remember that security can't solely be money or a physically attractive spouse. Money can be lost, and physical attractiveness can fade. Security begins first in your mind. Then when you recognize security, don't settle for anyone who would bring insecurity to a relationship.

Reflect

Ask yourself the following questions. Answer as honestly and thoughtfully as you can. Reflect on your answers, and use them to help you to prepare yourself to provide the security and protection your spouse needs or receive the security your spouse provides.

1. How do I define *security*?

2. What makes me feel most secure? Why?

3. (List those things that make you feel insecure.) What makes me feel insecure in these areas?

4. What things from my past am I holding on to that might affect my ability to provide security for or receive security from my spouse?

5. How have I prepared myself to provide security for my spouse?

— Chapter 4 —

Faithfulness

*"O love the L*ORD*, all ye his saints: for the L*ORD *preserveth the faithful, and plentifully rewardeth the proud doer."*
Psalm 31:23

At Niagara Falls, an acrobat prepared to walk a tight-rope over the rushing water below. To the people gathered around, he asked, "Do you believe I can walk to the other side on this tightrope?" The people said they believed he could, and they cheered him on. The acrobat successfully made the trip across and back.

Then, the acrobat asked the crowd if they thought he could cross the falls on the tightrope hopping on one leg. They answered a resounding yes and watched as the acrobat hopped across the falls and back, relieved that he had succeeded.

Next, the acrobat asked his adoring fans, "Do you believe I can go across, hopping on one leg, and rolling a wheelbarrow?" The crowd gasped, but they assured him that they believed he could do it. Then he asked, "Who will volunteer to sit in the wheelbarrow?"

Nobody got in the wheelbarrow.

Faithfulness is getting in the wheelbarrow. Faithfulness is knowing that in any relationship, it will feel like you're on only one leg, things are getting shaky, and you might get dumped out of the wheelbarrow at any minute. But you go full steam ahead anyway, trusting God's promises, because He's faithful.

Part of the process of becoming marriage material is learning how to be trustworthy, reliable, and faithful. It's becoming a person who is committed, a person who's going to be there, no matter what. And you can usually tell whether people are faithful while you're dating them.

You need to see where that person has been faithful in the past before you can trust that he or she will be faithful to you in the future. If a person can't be faithful in the most basic situations, then you're going to be disappointed in your relationship.

IN THE garden of Eden, God made Adam and Eve stewards of their new home and everything in it. God trusted them to follow His instructions and to faithfully take care of their home. We know that that didn't last long, but God expects the same from us: to be faithful to Him and to obey His commands.

God gives us assignments to complete and watches how we manage what He gives us, and He rewards our obedience and faithfulness. The psalmist said, "O love the LORD, all ye his saints: for the LORD perserveth the faithful, and plentifully rewardeth the proud doer" (Psalm 31:23). The psalmist could talk about God rewarding the faithful and the obedient because God is also faithful, so much so, that the psalmist had placed his own trust in God (Psalm 31:1).

In Psalm 128, the psalmist talks more about the rewards of the faithful: "Blessed is every one that feareth the LORD; that walketh in his ways" (Psalm 128:1). The person who honors and fears the Lord will walk in His ways and be faithful and obedient. The psalmist declares that that person will be blessed. Then he says that "thou shalt eat the labour of thine hands: happy shalt thou be, and it shall be well with thee" (Psalm 128:2). When you're faithful in your work and in your finances, you'll produce much fruit and be happy.

Those who are faithful will also see their families prosper: "Thy wife shall be as a fruitful vine by the sides of thine house: thy children like olive plants round about thy table" (Psalm 128:3). A vine clings, climbs, and cultivates; but it has to be nurtured and fed to do that. You can't expect your spouse to grow and flourish if you're not providing the right environment at home. If you've been unkind to your spouse all the time, you can't expect him or her to be loving, patient, and understanding when you're in the mood for intimacy. That shows a lack of faithfulness.

When the psalmist mentions that the children will be like olive plants, he's saying that a person has to be faithful in the care of the olive plants. It takes years for an olive plant to produce enough fruit to extract oil, so in the meantime, you have to take care of the plant. You can't abandon it simply because a year or so has gone by and you don't have enough fruit for oil. But if you keep nurturing the plant, you will eventually reap the benefits.

According to the psalmist, if you remain faithful, "the LORD shall bless thee out of Zion: and thou shalt see the good of Jerusalem all the days of thy life. Yea, thou shalt see thy children's children, and peace upon Israel" (Psalm 128:5-6).

FAITHFULNESS IS closely related to the concepts of reliability, trustworthiness, loyalty, and dependability. If the person you're dating hasn't kept his or her word about anything, don't think of giving that person a promotion to marriage. Or if you have had difficulty being reliable and faithful to anything, even in the most basic things, you need to better prepare yourself to be marriage material. It's unfair to promise to be faithful to someone when you can't keep your word to anyone else.

When the apostle Paul told the church in Ephesus that a man is to love his wife as Christ loves the church, first, he was emphasizing God's faithfulness to us. Then he was saying that since Christ has modeled His love and faithfulness for us, we're able to be faithful, too. So if you're struggling to figure out what faithfulness looks like, look at Christ. Look at how He loves His bride, the church. In fact, Christ loved us so much, He died for us! He gave His all. Over the last 2,000 years, the church hasn't always been faithful. We haven't always modeled love, but Christ is still faithful.

Jeremiah wrote of the greatness of God's faithfulness: "It is of the LORD's mercies that we are not consumed, because his compassions fail not. They are new every morning: great is thy faithfulness" (Lamentations 3:22-23). Every day we wake up, God is there, ready to give us new mercies. It doesn't matter how badly we messed up the day before. He's still there every morning, ready to give us new mercies.

That is the model you must keep before you as you prepare to get married. And if you're married, that is now your model of faithfulness to your spouse. Every morning your spouse wakes up, you should be there to wipe the slate clean and begin anew. It doesn't matter what happened the day before.

Maybe he burned the toast. Maybe she forgot to pay the electricity bill and the lights were turned off. He might have forgotten to gas up the car, and she might have distracted you when you wanted to watch the game. But remember God's faithfulness. Every morning, He's right there for you, offering you a brand-new start.

God's faithfulness doesn't wane because you get older or because He grows bored with you. Some relationships start off in a whirlwind of romance—flowers, expensive dinners, opening doors, daily texts. It's easy to love someone in the beginning because both people are putting their best foot forward. They're on their best behavior.

But after a few months or a few years, things get old and stale. There aren't as many bouquets of flowers coming or texts being sent saying "I love you." But as God does with us, every day should be a new day to show your love and affection. Be faithful in doing that, and you'll see your relationship blossom!

THE CONCEPT of faithfulness goes hand in hand with integrity. Who are you when no one else is around? Are you faithful to who you say you are? Are you one person at work, another person at church, and another person on vacation? Marriage requires that you develop integrity and be for your spouse who he or she needs you to be.

One day, I went grocery shopping and entered the bread aisle. I saw a woman grabbing loaves of bread by the armload and throwing them into her shopping cart. I thought that was strange, but I kept walking toward her.

As I got closer to the woman and her shopping cart, I could see that she was putting all those loaves of bread on top of a case of beer that was at the bottom of the cart. Obviously, she had recognized me as a preacher and thought she needed to hide the beer she was buying. I'm glad she respected me as a man of God, but I wonder if she ever stopped to think that God was in that aisle long before I got there.

A person who fears the Lord will walk in His ways, no matter who's looking. That's a person of integrity. Be faithful and obedient to the Lord, and live everyday as if you're in His presence—because you are.

HEBREWS 11:1 says, "Now faith is the substance of things hoped for, the evidence of things not seen." In relationships, sometimes you can't see anything. All you have is the promise God gave you, but you have to be faithful to that promise for it to be manifested.

The prophet Hosea married Gomer, a prostitute, because that's what God told him to do. So he had to commit himself to this person who had all kinds of challenges. She had children, but left them, so he had to raise them. Gomer was in the streets, but Hosea was committed to what God had told him. Hosea wasn't simply enduring a bad relationship because he couldn't do any better or because that's what he wanted for his life. He endured because God had a bigger agenda. Hosea's marriage was a picture of sinful Israel, and God was showing His people how they had been unfaithful to Him.

But God remained faithful. When Gomer left Hosea to be a slave to one of her lovers, God instructed Hosea to go and buy her back for 15 shekels and some barley. This showed God's faithfulness to Israel and His willingness to take them back. Through this relationship, we can see that if a man's love "can be so deep, how unfathomable must be the love of God."[1]

God calls us to a life of faithfulness, even when we have given up and can't see the use. In marriage, no spouse is perfect, and there will be times when God will lead you to forgive and wipe the slate clean.

Eighteen years ago, my wife and I separated. We had been going through some rough patches. While we were separated, I fathered a child out of wedlock. That brought me to the lowest point of my life.

I was ready to give up and commit suicide. I saw no reason to go on. My marriage was in shambles, and now I had this child, the tangible evidence of my unfaithfulness.

But my wife didn't give up on me. She said, "I know you're a good man, a good husband, and a good father. You've made a mistake, but I choose to characterize you by the condition of your heart, not by what you've done." She wasn't giving me a pass, though. She told me that I would need to repent and get right with God. She could forgive me, but the burden to rebuild our marriage and to earn her trust again was entirely on me.

Her forgiveness and willingness to give me another chance saved me. She was faithful to me and wiped the slate clean, which resurrected our marriage.

Today, my 18-year-old daughter lives with us and is ready to head to college because my wife didn't give up on me. God worked through her to make our family whole again.

My wife and I have shared our story all over the country, and I share it with you now to encourage you to be faithful but also to be forgiving. If you're struggling in that area, look to how faithful God is to each of us every single day. No matter what happened the day before or how far we've fallen, He stands ready to forgive us and help us start anew.

WHEN I was a child, my mother would tell us to hurry home after school because she was cooking pork chops and gravy, rice, peas, and biscuits—our favorite meal. My brother, who was older, would get home first and eat up the pork chops. Then he would tell me that my mother hadn't cooked them. He said all we had was rice and gravy, peas, and biscuits.

But I knew my brother was lying. I knew the difference between gravy when there's meat and when there's no meat. There was a completely different taste. I might not have seen those pork chops, but I knew they had been there. Eventually, he went to the bottom of the freezer where he'd hidden two chops, and he pulled them out.

As an adult, I laugh when I think of my brother's antics. But it's a good lesson for believing in God's faithfulness. When God makes promises, we might see the gravy, but we don't see the pork chops. But God is faithful. He's a promise-keeper, and we just have to trust that those pork chops are on the way!

Perhaps you don't see much in a person yet. You don't see a good communicator. You don't see a good provider. You don't see a good father yet. But you know you have the gravy. You have the substance of what you're hoping for.

Most people are waiting to meet "the perfect person." You won't meet that person because none of us is perfect. Everyone has issues or flaws of some kind.

When you enter a relationship, you enter by faith. You don't yet see everything that will unfold, so you have to trust God. Trust Him that even though you don't see everything yet, through the process of walking with God, and with time, you believe that eventually God's promise will come to pass.

If you're struggling with being faithful, consider the following:

Reflect on God's faithfulness. Despite Israel's waywardness, idol worship, and disobedience, God remained faithful to His people. And God is faithful to us today. When we stray, make mistakes, and disobey His Word, God is still there to help us, forgive us, and bless us because His faithfulness is not predicated on our goodness. The prophet Jeremiah said, "It is of the LORD's mercies that we are not consumed, because his compassions fail not. They are new every morning: great is thy faithfulness"

(Lamentations 3:22-23). Seek to follow God's example of faithfulness in your relationships.

Examine where you are now in your journey of faithfulness. Are you trustworthy? Are you a person of integrity who keeps your word? Can others rely on you to be there for them? Work on being faithful in small areas, and then stretch to be faithful in larger areas. Don't make promises you can't keep, but strive to keep the promises you make.

Be willing to forgive. It's no secret. Human beings make mistakes. Sometimes we fail. And when we fail, sometimes we hurt other people. But part of being faithful in marriage is being willing to be patient when your spouse makes mistakes.

When we fail God and stray from His Word, He always stands ready to forgive us. So if we're modeling God's faithfulness to our spouses, then we have to stand ready to forgive, too. (I'm not advocating that you withstand abuse or mistreatment. That's another issue that needs to be dealt with through legal channels and whatever it takes for your safety.)

But when it comes to the typical issues that couples face, I'm simply asking you to forgive your spouse when he or she messes up. Be faithful to your spouse. Give him or her a clean slate so that together you can work to fix your relationship, restore the broken trust, and heal the wounds.

Reflect

Ask yourself the following questions. Answer as honestly and thoughtfully as you can. Reflect on your answers, and use them to help you prepare to be faithful in your relationship.

1. Where have I seen faithfulness modeled out effectively? What can I extract from that experience that I can use in learning to be faithful?

2. What have I been faithful to that has prepared me to be marriage material?

3. How does God's faithfulness help me to be faithful in relationships?

4. If I'm unfaithful, what causes me to be unfaithful?

5. What traits do I look for in a faithful person?

– Chapter 5 –

Vision

"Where there is no vision, the people perish: but he that keepeth the law, happy is he." Proverbs 29:17-19

An important key to choosing the right mate is having vision, spiritual vision, that is. When you look at that person, what do you see with your spiritual eye? What do you see in that person that you're believing God for?

The writer of Proverbs wasn't exaggerating when he said, "Where there is no vision, the people perish." Without vision, relationships languish, dry up, and eventually die. That's because there isn't a common focus that moves it forward.

God has a plan for each person, but He also has a plan for couples. And His plan is best manifested through a common vision. So it's important for you to seek divine vision as you prepare to become marriage material.

WHEN LOOKING at a potential mate, what is your vision and what is that person's vision? Do you have common or opposing goals?

In 2 Kings, the writer tells us about the interaction between the prophet Elijah and his protégé, Elisha. After Elijah had spent time with Elisha, he said, "Ask what I shall do for thee, before I be taken away from thee" (2 Kings 2:9). Elisha then asked the prophet for "a double portion of thy spirit [to] be upon me" (2 Kings 2:9). Elijah responded, "Thou hast asked a hard thing: nevertheless, if thou *see* me when I am taken from thee, it shall be so unto thee; but if not, it shall not be so" (2 Kings 2:10, italics added).

Basically, Elijah was telling Elisha, "If you can see what I see, then you will have what you ask for. If not, then you won't receive it." A potential mate should share what's in your vision. If he or she doesn't have in the spiritual eye what you have, it will be difficult for that person to see what you see.

It's so important in relationships to believe that God will connect you with someone with the same thing in his or her eye that God has put in your eye. The prophet Amos wrote, "Can two walk together, except they be agreed?" (Amos 3:3). And the agreement has to come about as it relates to vision. Wherever there is not proper vision, there will always be division.

Someday, when someone comes to me asking for my daughter's hand in marriage, the first question I'm going to ask him is, "Where's your vision? Where are you going?" And if he tells me he doesn't know, then that's the time to get the baseball bat and chase him off the steps! If he doesn't know where he's going, then he's not going to be able to lead my daughter anywhere.

Proverbs 29:18 says, "Where there is no vision, the people perish." The amplified version of that verse says, "Without a redemptive picture of Christ, the people perish." So it's not just having a vision about a big house and a job. There's nothing wrong with those things, but true vision includes seeing the finished work of Christ and God's purposes for us. We can't coexist in a way that brings glory to God and edify each other if we don't have that type of vision.

Where there's no vision, then dreams, hope, and goals die. Where there is no vision, there's going to be division. When you see something and your spouse doesn't, you're divided and not in agreement, so there's no support or unity in that relationship.

If you're thinking about being with someone who doesn't see Jesus as the Son of God and that He is the only means of salvation, then you're trying to connect with someone who's blind and won't appreciate your spiritual vision. It's tempting to settle for someone because you're tired of waiting or you're giving into your flesh. But God wants you to wait on His promise and wait for the person who can value your vision. If that person can't see what you see, if they can't value your vision, they won't value you.

SAMSON'S LIFE was in chaos. His marriage had ended in divorce, and he was visiting prostitutes (Judges 16). But when he met Delilah, something changed. The Bible doesn't tell us what Delilah looked like, but she seemed to know how to talk to Samson.

Samson had had sex before, so that wasn't his weakness. But no one had ever tapped into his inner man, his inner ego, like Delilah did. She simply said, "Samson, what makes you so strong?"

Another important thing Delilah did was she gave Samson a place to rest in her lap. It was the wrong place to rest because Delilah meant him no good, but that's where he was. He trusted a woman who did not have a shared vision, because his ultimate purpose was to deliver the children of Israel from the Philistines. Instead, he was spending time with a woman who was paid to deliver him over to those same Philistines. So if you're dating someone, and you suspect that his or her vision is to destroy you spiritually, emotionally, physically, or financially, run away now!

Matthew 6:21 says, "Where your treasure is, there will your heart be also." The person you tell your secrets to will also have your heart. It's dangerous to hand your heart to somebody who doesn't share your vision. You're making yourself vulnerable for any kind of attack.

Finally, Samson told Delilah where his strength was, in his hair, and she immediately told the Philistines. Because of his Nazarite vows, Samson held strength in his hair, which symbolized the vows he'd made to God. But he had given up his commitment to God. And the first thing the Philistines did upon capturing Samson was to put out his eyes. People who don't value your vision, will try to extinguish yours.

WHEN JESUS walked on the water to his disciples' boat, at first, they thought He was a ghost (Matthew 14:26). But this is why perspective and vision are so important. Peter recognized Jesus and asked if he, too, could join Him on the water. From the disciples' perspective, they saw a spirit, a ghost, walking toward them. How else could what they saw be walking on water? But from Peter's perspective, he saw his Lord, One who could do anything—even walk on water.

When people quote this passage of Scripture, they often say Peter stepped out on the water. Actually, Peter stepped out on Jesus' word. And because he had the proper vision as it related to Jesus, he could walk on places others could not.

There's a difference between boat-riders and water-walkers. And so, in relationships, how far you go will depend on what you see and what your spouse sees. Are you willing to walk out on God's word to fulfill your vision? Or are you satisfied to ride safely in the boat but with no vision?

If you see your potential husband trying to fulfill God's promise but you don't think he'll ever become anything, then your vision of him is small and will make him small. If you are impatient with where your potential wife is trying to go in God, then your vision of her won't help her get there.

You've got to connect with someone who has the right perception, because you don't want to spend 20 years in a miserable relationship on the boat, never experiencing anything supernatural or divine. If you want to walk on water, then get with someone who has the proper perspectives of Christ and what you can do together in Christ, with no boundaries and no limits.

THE OPPOSITE of blindness is vision, but we know from the Bible that Jesus can heal blindness. When Jesus restored people's sight, many times, He wasn't just healing them of physical blindness. He was also giving them spiritual sight into who He is and His great power.

When you're preparing yourself for marriage, make sure you have spiritual sight that is 20/20, but also look for a potential mate who has spiritual insight and discernment, someone who can see more than just what's on the surface. Together, you can see the heart of God and His purposes. Then you can have shared vision, and you can be unified in that vision.

I've shared with you how my wife encouraged me to think bigger and to expand my vision. We went from a congregation of 100 to 500, and we needed a bigger place to meet. Although I would have settled for the 700-seat banquet hall, my wife wouldn't let me limit the vision.

We ended up at the 5,000-seat Memorial Auditorium, the largest venue in Chattanooga! And within a few months, we were putting out chairs in the aisles. Everything my wife said about growing my vision came to pass.

I thank God for my wife being in my life because she could see when it was difficult for me to see. There will be times when your spiritual eyes will become cloudy. You won't be able to see what God has promised, so it's important to be in a relationship with someone who can see when you can't see, who can keep nudging you until your sight is restored.

The problem with Samson was that he had vision, but he got involved with someone who didn't value that vision and had a plan to destroy it. So having a vision alone is not enough. You need to partner with someone who can see that vision, too, and can help you as it is being manifested.

HAVING VISION goes deeper than just having goals. Couples who have goals can meet those and still feel unfulfilled and empty. God-given vision in marriage should serve to help couples focus on the bigger picture: serving Christ and doing together what they can't do alone. Having this kind of vision causes a couple to dig deep and bring their lives and relationship into alignment with God's Word and His plan and purpose for their marriage.

On his website, Marriage Today, Pastor Jimmy Evans says that there are five reasons vision in marriage is extremely important. First, vision gives *clarity*. If husbands and wives aren't clear on why they're together and what God's plan and purpose for them is, then it will be difficult to hold their relationships together.

Second, vision provides *energy and passion*. When you know what direction you're going in, it's easier to get excited about it. However, with no vision, it can feel as if you're both drifting aimlessly through life, merely existing but with no specific purpose or direction.

Third, vision allows couples to live in *purity*. Without vision, there are no guidelines or ground rules for how you will live together and treat each other. You then become susceptible to any and every negative influence around you. But with vision, you establish boundaries that will keep negative influences from entering your marriage, while within your marriage you are making sure that you honor each other in the way God intended.

Fourth, vision produces *unity*. Evans says, "Couples fight because they don't see eye-to-eye. They have competing visions—that's what the word *division* means. Two people can't walk together unless they're in agreement." Unity dispels division, which is the enemy of any marriage. A couple should have a "single vision" so they can "have the same focus."

Finally, vision is *victory*! A united couple is going to be more successful and win more victories together than a divided couple. And as they move from one phase of their relationship to the next, as they achieve their shared goals, they will be victorious.[1]

TO HELP you develop your spiritual vision, consider the following:

Sharpen your vision. Before you can share your vision with someone else, make sure your vision is as sharp as it can be. Be alone with God, and spend time in His Word so that you can have clarity before you impart your vision to someone else. If your vision has been blurry, ask God to correct it.

Let the Holy Spirit be your GPS. With God's Spirit, you can know what direction you're supposed to be traveling, and your potential spouse should be going in the same direction. Ruth chose to travel with Naomi to Bethlehem, but Orpah decided to go back toward Moab. Orpah's vision didn't match that of Ruth and Naomi.

Work on a shared vision. To get to a place of shared vision, you and your spouse have to get past surface things. Physical attraction, money, and material things are fine, but your godly purpose is deeper than that. Pray and ask God to help you find areas where your vision meshes with your potential spouse's. Think past today. Look at long-term plans. Ask, What are you believing God for?

Reflect

Ask yourself the following questions. Answer as honestly and thoughtfully as you can. Reflect on your answers, and use them to help you to define your vision and work on a shared vision with your potential spouse.

1. How do I define *vision*?

2. What is my vision?

3. How does my relationship with God influence my vision?

4. What is my experience with people who lack vision?

5. How can I improve my vision? How can I help my spouse improve his or her vision?

– Chapter 6 –

Submission

"Giving thanks always for all things unto God and the Father in the name of our Lord Jesus Christ; submitting yourselves one to another in the fear of God." Ephesians 5:20-22

When you hear the word *submission*, what is your first thought? Probably not a good one. Our society has always promoted a "me first" ideology that clashes with God's commands to put others first, therefore it has poisoned the concept of living a submitted life to God or to anyone else. But despite how the world defines it, *submission* doesn't mean inferiority or that a person is less-than. In God's economy, submission is so much more.

But we don't just submit ourselves in marriage. We submit ourselves to someone every day—parents, employers, government. But what does God say about submission? And how is submitting oneself part of preparing to be marriage material?

JESUS KNEW His time was short, so during the feast of the Passover, He gathered His disciples for one final meal. After their last supper together, Jesus rose "from supper, and laid aside his garments; and took a towel, and girded himself. . . . and began to wash the disciples' feet" (John 13:4-5). How could this be? How could the Lord of heaven humble Himself to wash someone else's feet?

In ancient times, people typically wore sandals and walked wherever they went, so by the time they arrived at their destination, their feet were dirty. It was a sign of hospitality to provide water and towels for your guests to wash their feet, but for servants to wash the guests' feet meant they were taking on one of the lowliest, dirtiest jobs in the household.

Before the Last Supper, the disciples had been arguing about who would be the greatest in the Kingdom. They wanted to know who would sit where, on Jesus' left or right. But now, just before He was to face His death, Jesus quietly took up the towel, poured the water, and knelt at their feet.

Jesus's disciples must have been shocked to see Him put Himself in such a vulnerable position. Peter was so taken aback that he said, "Thou shalt *never* wash my feet" (John 13:8, italics added). But Jesus educated Peter quickly in the concept of fellowship: "If I wash thee not, thou hast no part with me" (John 13:8).

After washing the feet of all the disciples, Jesus taught them about servant-leadership, saying, "If I then, your Lord and Master, have washed your feet; ye also ought to wash one another's feet. For I have given you an example, that ye should do as I have done to you" (John 13:14-15). This is a beautiful illustrated sermon on submission. Jesus could humble Himself and wash the disciples' feet because He knew exactly Who He was and what His purpose was, so He wasn't too insecure to kneel before His friends and wash their dirty feet. And He wasn't going to lose a thing by performing the lowly task.

Philippians 2:5-10 says:

Let this mind be in you, which was also in Christ Jesus: Who, being in the form of God, thought it not robbery to be equal with God: But made himself of no reputation, and took upon him the form of a servant, and was made in the likeness of men:

And being found in fashion as a man, he humbled himself, and became obedient unto death, even the death of the cross. Wherefore God also hath highly exalted him, and given him a name which is above every name: That at the name of Jesus every knee should bow, of things in heaven, and things in earth, and things under the earth. And that every tongue should confess that Jesus Christ is Lord, to the glory of God the Father.

Paul is showing us that as great as Jesus is, He didn't hesitate to humble Himself, even unto death. And after He humbled Himself, "God . . . highly exalted him." By taking the form of a servant, Jesus didn't lose anything. He didn't stop being the King of kings and Lord or lords. This is how Jesus modeled submission for us. It's why we don't have to be afraid of losing anything (except for our pride) and appearing weak.

As a pastor, I take Jesus' message to heart. Members of my congregation will often find me sweeping or mopping the floors of the church, and they want to immediately grab the broom or mop and do it for me. But I tell them that as a leader, I have to demonstrate leadership through my service. You can't become a leader and do less. The Bible says, "For unto whomsoever much is given, of him shall be much required: and to whom men have committed much, of him they will ask the more" (Luke 12:48). The more God blesses you with, the more He expects out of you. So, I exemplify my ability to lead by my ability to serve.

Often, we bristle at submitting ourselves for two reasons. First, many of us don't know who we are or Who we belong to. We haven't found our true identity in Christ or in our natural lives. Second, we harbor deep insecurities that cause us to be afraid to put ourselves in vulnerable positions. We fear that if we submit to someone, that person will take advantage of us or abuse us in some way. We believe that it makes us appear less-than if we humble ourselves and serve others. But Jesus proved that He could be great and still serve. He could wash the disciples' feet and still be the Son of God.

IT'S FITTING that in the verse before the apostle Paul wrote directing wives to submit to their husbands, he wrote, "Submitting yourselves *one to another* in the fear of God" (Ephesians 5:21, italics added). This means that each spouse is to submit to each other. Most people go straight for verse 22 and try to badger women about submitting, but Paul had something else in mind. By telling us to submit to each other, he's saying that no one gets a pass on submitting. It's not just for women!

Luke wrote about a centurion soldier who needed Jesus' help. The centurion's servant, who was dear to him, was near death. He had heard about Jesus and all the miracles He had performed, so he sent for Jesus, begging Him to come and heal his servant. When Jesus was near the centurion's house, the soldier sent word, saying, "Lord, . . . I am not worthy that thou shouldest enter under my roof: Wherefore neither thought I myself worthy to come unto thee. . . . For I also am a man set under authority, having under me soldiers, and I say unto one, Go, and he goeth; and to another, Come, and he cometh; and to my servant, do this, and he doeth it" (Luke 7:6-7).

A centurion was roughly equivalent to a captain in the military, and he led a company of 100 soldiers. So this man, as he told Jesus, was used to giving orders and having them obeyed. But once Jesus was near, the centurion humbled himself before the Lord and submitted to Him. Even Jesus marveled at the man's humility, and He gave the centurion the miracle he asked for because he understood submission. In fact, the centurion understood submission from both sides of the equation, and he didn't cease to be in command of his soldiers simply because he submitted himself to Jesus.

WHEN PAUL addresses women on the subject of submission, he follows it up immediately with "For the husband is the head of the wife, even as Christ is the head of the church: and he is the saviour of the body" (Ephesians 5:23). This places a huge responsibility on husbands. If they are to be the head of their wives as Christ is the head of the church, they have to remember all of the things Christ has done for the church, including death.

As the saying goes, "Heavy is the head that wears the crown." Since the husband is the head, he shoulders the responsibility to serve because Jesus said, "He that is greatest among you shall be your servant" (Matthew 23:10-12). Being the head isn't about ordering your wife around and making her do everything around the house while you have your feet propped up, watching TV. Jesus is telling us that it's about fellowship, serving and then being served.

In Ephesians 5, Paul is clearly talking about Christ and the church, but he's giving us an example of how that potential relationship will work if you follow this model. The church looks to Christ as priest, provider, protector, prophet, and head. The woman looks to the man as the head. The church has to submit to Christ. By faith, we have to obey.

When I speak at marriage conferences, men are quick to encourage me to talk at length about submission. They tell me, "Make sure you talk about submission!" "Tell my wife she needs to submit to me. Tell her she needs to give me more." "Straighten her out!" I ask them if they're sure they want me to talk about submission, and they always answer yes.

But when I stand up to speak, I start with 1 Corinthians 11:3: "I would have you know, that the head of every man is Christ; and the head of the woman is the man; and the head of Christ is God." Paul is setting up a structure that, when all parts are aligned, functions as God designed it. So I'm sure those men were pretty disappointed when I pointed out to them that though they are in authority at home, they are also *under* authority to God. Which means God has certain expectations of them that they are required to meet, too.

While they're complaining about what their wives aren't doing, God is saying, "I'm having the same problem with you. You won't talk to Me. You won't listen to Me. You won't give Me anything. Perhaps if you address your intimacy on My level first, and submit to Me first, then maybe your wife will have a clearer picture of what submission should look like." So husbands have to model submission to show that they understand servant-leadership and can be accountable to someone, too.

NOW TO the verses many women dread to hear: "Wives, submit yourselves unto your own husbands, as unto the Lord" (Ephesians 5:22). "Wives, submit yourselves unto your own husbands, as it is fit in the Lord" (Colossians 3:18). Lest you think this is just one of Paul's idiosyncrasies, let's look back at Abraham and Sarah. Sarah called Abraham "lord" (small *l*), a title of honor, signifying that she thought of him as her head and master and that she respected God's order.

Remember, when the Bible talks about submission, it's talking about the military use of the term. In the military, to submit is to stay in your rank. For example, if a battalion is marching, the soldiers need to stay in the order of their rank. So to bring that into the context of marriage, to submit would be to stay in line with what God is telling you to do. Respect the order God has established, and fulfill your role within that structure.

Two of the most common questions women ask me about submission are, "What if a man is not doing what he's supposed to do? Does the woman still have to submit?" My response is yes and no. Yes, the woman still has to submit as long as the man is not trying to make the woman do anything against God. She still should respect God's order in her home. But, no, the woman doesn't have to submit to the man if what he is trying to make her do is contrary to God. In that case, the couple needs serious counseling, which is another area all together.

There will be times when God will want you to submit, or go under (*sub* = under), so God can reach the man's heart. Sometimes God wants you to duck under, or get out of the way, so He can handle the situation, because He can do it better than you can. If you're too busy going toe-to-toe with your husband, you place yourself in the way, and God can't reach him through your anger. But when you submit, God has a straight line to his heart.

Some women are too insecure to submit. Before marriage, they have gotten college degrees, established careers, traveled, and become successful; and they are afraid that to submit would mean they're going to have to become their husband's servant and they will be seen as weak and dependent. But to submit requires a lot of strength because it goes against our normal human pride and ego.

A submitted person isn't insecure or afraid of being seen as weak. She knows exactly who she is, and she understands what God says about submission and how Jesus first modeled it for us when He knelt before His disciples to wash their feet.

FIRST PETER 3 makes it clear that while men and women stand equal before God, they are still different. While Peter tells women to "be in subjection to your own husbands," he also tells men that they are to "dwell with [their wives] according to knowledge, giving honour unto the wife, as unto the weaker vessel" (1 Peter 3:1, 7). Peter isn't saying that women are weak in ability or intelligence. He's simply emphasizing how God created men and women differently physically and emotionally.

Ultimately, we are saved because Jesus submitted to the will of His Father. He submitted Himself to a horrible death just so that we might have salvation. Yet, today, Christ sits at the right hand of the Father and has lost none of His power.

Submission should be mutual between two spouses. It's not one-sided at all. And to submit is not to be inferior, but it is to put the needs of your spouse before your own. If you're still self-centered and worrying about meeting your own needs, then that's almost the same as being single. But if the husband and the wife are submitting to each other and putting the needs of the other above his or her own, then both will have their needs met. But that all starts with being fully and wholly submitted to God and following the order that He has ordained.

Whether you are a man or a woman, the key to a submitted life is the Holy Spirit. There are some things that we just can't accomplish in our flesh. We need the supernatural power of God's Spirit to help us. And by submitting to the Holy Spirit working in us and through us, we will find that what we've resisted becomes easier for us to do.

SUBMISSION IS a quality trait that has to be learned and developed. Most of us learn a basic form of submission as children as we submit to our parents. Then we learn to submit to authority at school with teachers and principals. At work, we submit to our employers; and at church, we submit to our pastors and spiritual leaders.

The worst way to learn how to be submitted is always getting what you want when you want it. When you get your first job at a fast-food restaurant, you can't go in demanding that they put you on fries. That's not how it works. And you can't quit because you didn't get your way. I want to raise my daughter so the man she marries doesn't have a difficult time living with her because she's so spoiled and used to getting her way. Parents who spoil their children are setting them up for failure, especially when they get married.

But even those in authority should know how to submit. I'm a pastor and a bishop, but I honor those working in the church in their various capacities.

Recently, we've been remodeling our building, and we have a committee that makes certain decisions about interior decoration. A committee member asked me what color I wanted the floor to be. I had my preference, but I had been outvoted by the committee. As pastor, I could have vetoed their decision, pulling rank and throwing my weight around. But as I often say, there's safety in the multitude of counsel. And since the committee voted for another color, then I told them it was a great idea.

To be a leader doesn't mean you can't be submitted. And if you're submitted, it doesn't mean you're inferior. If you're struggling with submission, look at the Scriptures for the example Jesus modeled for us.

∞

IF YOU need to work on being submitted in your relationships, consider the following:

Look at where you are right now. Reflect on where you are right now in living a submitted life. Think about whether you're submitted in some areas but not others. Look for areas where you can improve.

Read God's Word and pray. Read the passages of Scripture mentioned in this chapter, and meditate on them. Pray that God will allow His Word to penetrate your spirit and help you to have a desire to submit to Him first and then to your spouse.

Don't allow society to define submission for you. We live in a world where society is in direct opposition to God and His Word. They have redefined words to mean something other than what they mean; and in so doing, many people are living in rebellion to God. Seek God for answers on how you are to submit yourself. Don't let society's worldview poison your heart and spirit against what God is telling you to do.

Employ the power of the Holy Spirit. For many people, submitting themselves is hard because it forces them to face deep-seated insecurities and fears when putting themselves in such a vulnerable position. But call on God's power and His Spirit to help you get to a point where you can submit without fear.

Reflect

Ask yourself the following questions. Answer as honestly and thoughtfully as you can. Reflect on your answers, and use them to help you learn how to submit yourself to one another.

1. Before reading this chapter, what did I think about submission? After reading the chapter, have my views changed? If so, how so?

2. If I'm struggling with submitting, what keeps me from submitting myself?

3. In what areas do I need to submit in my relationship with God?

4. In what areas do I need to submit to my spouse?

5. How does submission in relationships line up with God's Word?

— Chapter 7 —

Trust

"[Jesus] said to Simon, Launch out into the deep, and let down your nets for a draught." Luke 5:4

In Matthew 7:24-29, Jesus talks about building one's house on sand or on rock. The obvious takeaway is, don't build a house on stand because it will fall. But many people miss the subtle point Jesus was making.

The wise man and the foolish man both built houses, but the strength of their houses' foundations wasn't revealed until a storm came. Since the house built on sand was built on something that's ever shifting and changing, that house fell; while the house built on rock was built on something more permanent and lasting, so it withstood the storm.

The Bible doesn't mention what either house looked like, but it's probably a sure bet that both houses looked just fine. But despite what they may have looked like, when the storm came, it revealed how strong each one was.

It's the same with relationships. There's nothing wrong with wanting a physically attractive spouse. Neither is it wrong for us to look at other people's relationships that appear to be successful and want our relationships to look like theirs. But if our relationships aren't built on a solid foundation, they are doomed to fail.

Trust should be one of the key building blocks of any relationship's foundation. If trust is missing, the relationship will eventually fall apart. But if we build on a solid-rock reliance on God, knowing that we are open and honest with each other, then we're establishing a good foundation for our relationships.

TRUSTING OTHER people is difficult, especially because we know that human beings are flawed and capable of failing us. It's also hard to trust people, especially when we've experienced hurt in past relationships because we trusted too easily or were naïve in who we trusted. But the path to deeper trust in our spouses begins by trusting Jesus Christ and following His directions.

Luke 5:1-11 tells us that Jesus met up with Peter as he was putting away his boats and fishing nets. Peter, a professional fisherman, had been fishing all night and had caught nothing—not one fish. But Jesus told him to "launch out into the deep" and get ready for a great harvest of fish. In other words, Jesus was saying, "Even though you didn't catch a thing last night, even though you're frustrated with the empty net, I still want you to trust me."

Remember, Peter was a professional. Fishing wasn't his weekend hobby or something he did from time to time. This was his livelihood. However, Jesus wasn't a fisherman; but He is the Lord of heaven, and He knew what Peter did not know.

Bible scholars say that Peter didn't necessarily believe that Jesus knew what He was talking about or trust that he would catch anything. When there aren't any fish to be caught or they're out of the net's reach, there's not much a fisherman can do. Scholars believe that Peter went along with Jesus' plan, perhaps out of respect, or maybe he was just humoring his friend.

But when Peter was obedient, he and his crew caught so many fish that they needed more than one boat to haul in their catch. Once Peter saw that Jesus was right, he then repented of his unbelief. We can be confident that what Jesus tells us is always true. We can trust Him and trust His Word.

Sometimes that becomes the key in our relationships. When we trust the Lord, we trust His word and what He tells us to do. When you seek Him for direction and for the person you should be dating, you can be confident that when He steers you to a particular person, this is a person you can trust. That person won't be perfect and without flaws, but he or she will be the person best suited for you.

And when you experience ups and downs in your relationship, and you don't see much, God is telling you to go back out to where you were before, out into the deep, and trust Him that your relationship is going to be successful. That's when He's calling you to walk by faith and not by sight.

RECENTLY, I stayed at a resort and was looking forward to doing some fishing, but the fishing wasn't that challenging. I put my bait on the hook, threw my line into the shallow water, and then watched as the fish swam up to the hook and bit it. I didn't have to trust my bait or have faith that something would happen underwater because I could see everything in the shallows where I was standing. If I'd wanted to, I probably could have gotten a net and just scooped the fish out of the water.

Many of us have a shallow-water relationship with God. We only live by sight, which doesn't require us to have any faith. This type of faith doesn't help us to develop the trust we need when times get tough. But when God tells us to launch out into the deep, as He told Peter to do, that requires us to have faith because we can't see into the depths of the sea. Only God knows what's below the surface, so we have to trust Him to see where we can't see and to know what we don't know.

WHEN THE angel Gabriel appeared to Mary and said, "Behold, thou shalt conceive in thy womb, and bring forth a son" (Luke 2:31), Joseph wasn't there. In the beginning, he didn't get a personal announcement of what was about to take place. All he knew was that he was betrothed to Mary, they had not had sex, and they were to be married. But then she told him she was pregnant. Talk about trust!

At first, Joseph was unsure what to do, but he knew he didn't want Mary to be scandalized and punished. He thought he would "put her away privily" (Matthew 1:19) to spare her the embarrassment, shame, and ridicule. But an angel appeared to him and confirmed that Mary's pregnancy was "of the Holy Ghost" (Matthew 1:20). Joseph proved to be a just and honest man who could support

Mary. He was called and anointed to handle Mary's situation. Most men wouldn't have been able to.

We can't trust everyone to be able to handle our circumstances. Gabriel revealed God's plan to Mary, and then an angel shared it with Joseph. The trust they had was all predicated upon the word of God, and they had an agreement in that word.

One of the reasons many couples struggle with trust is because they have physical attraction and intellectual stimulation in their relationships, but they're lacking spiritual agreement. They don't have the raw ingredients for sustaining their relationship when times are tough or when they can't see what's going to happen next. But God is asking us to trust Him first and then work on trusting those He puts in our lives.

IF YOU can't trust a person while you're dating, why should you promote him or her to a higher level of covenant in marriage and think that that person is going to change? Someone once said that when people show you who they are the first time, believe them. You can tell a tree by the fruit it bears, so there's no way an apple tree should be able to fool you into thinking it's a peach tree once you see the fruit.

When you are in a relationship, look for evidence that the person is trustworthy and honest. If you're not seeing that and no amount of discussion is producing it, then it's time to leave.

Another term for dating is *courting*. When two people are courting, they're putting each other on trial. But if you take someone to trial, the worst person to put on the stand to tell you about that person is that same person, because he or she is going to tell you only the good things, not the bad. And if that person is only going to tell you the good things about himself or herself, then you're not getting the full picture.

More than likely, people aren't going to volunteer information about their anger issues, trust issues, insecurities, and hang-ups. In fact, while they're dating, they're probably going to be on their best behavior as much as possible—at least until they feel confident that they've sealed the deal. That's not a good environment for developing trust.

This type of dishonesty breeds contempt later on. Six months into the relationship and you find out this person is not the person you thought he or she was, you're right. You never got to meet the real person. They were so busy pretending to be someone else that they didn't show you who they really are.

WHEN MY wife and I first began dating, I would visit her at her parents' house, and it was like going to visit the Waltons, that large, friendly family from the 1970s show. There were at least 15 people living in that small house, and they would all come out and shake my hand, hug me, and ask me questions. If I was taking her out to dinner, they would ask me what time we'd be back, and then they would hug and kiss her and pray over her. I thought, *We're just going down the street!* To me, their behavior was weird and way over the top.

In contrast, when my wife would visit my mother's house, things were completely different. I lived with my mother, my brother, and my sister. That was it. And we were pretty quiet, compared to her family, and we didn't show much emotion, so there weren't any long, dramatic goodbyes or a list of questions. There also wasn't a lot of hugging and kissing.

As my wife and I were talking about getting married, she would say "Kevin, I love you!" over and over again. The most I would say is "Cool." But that would just prompt her to ask me if I loved her. Of course, I did, but I just didn't want to have to *say* it. But she wanted to hear me say it.

Then one day, she asked, "Why can't you express your emotions?" When I couldn't come up with an acceptable answer, she said, "I'm going to help you with that."

So I began to express my emotions to her. At the time, I was in my 20s, but I had never heard my mother tell me that she loved me, and I had never told her. We knew we loved each other, but we just had never said it.

My wife and I came from totally different backgrounds, and we had to bring our two histories together by being honest with each other. Telling her about how I express myself helped her understand why it wasn't easy for me to tell her I loved her. If I hadn't trusted her enough to share that knowledge with her, that would have created an obstacle for us, and she wouldn't have understood why it was so hard for me to be open.

When you don't know where a person is coming from emotionally, then you don't understand why he or she tenses up when you crack a fat joke or harp on money issues. But once you understand that person's history and he or she trusts you enough to be open and honest, then you know better how to love that person.

IF YOU'RE working on trust in relationships, consider the following:

Trust God. As human beings, we sometimes find it hard to trust what we don't see, what we can't touch. But when we are in relationship with God, that's one of the first things He asks us to do. We have to trust that God is all-mighty, all-powerful, and all-wise and is in control of all things. Only when we can trust Him and rest in His faithfulness can we learn to be open and trustworthy ourselves.

Be trustworthy in all things, not just in relationships. If you're not trustworthy at work, on your taxes, or with your parents, then you'll eventually find it easy to be untrustworthy in relationships, too. Your dishonesty in other areas will eventually corrode your honesty where it counts.

Pray and ask God to help you to be a person of integrity. There are some things that we can do only through the power of the Holy Spirit. So if you're struggling with being trustworthy, or you're finding it difficult to trust other people, pray about it, and invite the Holy Spirit to help you to become a person of integrity.

Reflect

Ask yourself the following questions. Answer as honestly and thoughtfully as you can. Reflect on your answers, and use them to help you learn how to trust.

1. Do I trust God? Why or why not? If not, what can I do to begin trusting God?

2. Do I struggle with trust issues? What is my history of trusting others?

3. When it comes to trust, what are my deal-breakers?

4. Are there areas of my life where I can't be open with my spouse, or potential spouse? Why not?

5. What can I do to be trustworthy?

– Chapter 8 –

Honesty

"If we confess our sins, he is faithful and just to forgive us our sins, and to cleanse us from all unrighteousness."
1 John 1:9

The saying goes, "Confession is good for the soul." There's something about being honest, being transparent, and coming clean that makes us feel better and lightens our burdens.

First John 1:9 says, "If we confess our sins, he is faithful and just to forgive us our sins." In other words, if we are honest with God, He will, in turn, forgive us and cleanse us. But the psalmist said that "when [he] kept silence," or wasn't honest with God, "[his] bones waxed old." So he decided to confess: "I acknowledge my sin unto thee, and mine iniquity have I not hid. I said, I will confess my transgressions unto the LORD; and thou forgavest the iniquity of my sin" (Psalm 32:3, 5).

God wants us to be honest with Him, but He also wants us to be honest and open in all of our relationships. Marriage requires honesty, or a husband and wife can't trust each other. And if there's no trust, the foundation of that marriage is built on sand and will eventually fall.

WHEN JOHN wrote about confession (1 John 1:9), he was showing us that being honest with God means putting aside all excuses and emotional crutches we may use to justify sinful behavior. Being honest in relationships means being open and transparent about where we've messed up, what we've done wrong. What it doesn't mean is hiding behind excuses and blaming other people when we make mistakes.

We can't use our dysfunctional childhoods, our parents' mistakes, or bad past relationships to excuse why we've messed up. You've probably heard these excuses, or used them yourself: "I came from a dysfunctional family." "I've got my mother's anger." "I've just always been this way." "My ex did me wrong, so now I don't trust anybody." These excuses don't allow us to be honest with others, and they don't allow us to be honest with ourselves. They only serve to justify our actions and avoid the hard work of improving ourselves and learning how to be more honest.

Sometimes our greatest struggle is being honest with ourselves. We've gone for so long overlooking our own mistakes that we've come to believe we don't have any faults. But 1 John 1:8 says, "If we say that we have no sin, we deceive ourselves, and the truth is not in us." John shows us that it's common for people to be dishonest with themselves when it relates to their own sin. It's part of our human nature. That was evident with Adam and Eve in the garden of Eden.

After they had sinned and had hidden themselves (as if they could hide from God!), the Lord asked Adam, "Where art thou?" The Creator God wasn't asking Adam where he was because God was somehow confused and couldn't find Adam. Instead, God was calling out Adam and his dishonesty. And soon after, Adam began the blame game. Instead of taking responsibility for his sin, he blamed Eve, who in turn blamed the serpent. Adam and Eve tried to justify their sin before God, and they couldn't be honest about what happened.

In the New Testament, another couple, Ananias and Saphira, showed how ego and pride can cause people to be dishonest with others. As the early church was being established, the believers "were of one heart and of one soul. . . . They had all things common" (Acts 4:32). So they came together, sold their houses and land so that everyone could have what they needed, and brought the proceeds to the apostles.

However, Ananias and Saphira decided that they wouldn't sell all that they had. They wanted to keep some back for themselves. That's not where their mistake was, though. No one required them to sell all of their possessions. Their mistake, however, was in lying to Peter and saying that they had sold all. But it's the last thing Peter said to Ananias that is so haunting and relevant today: "Thou hast not lied unto men, but unto God" (Acts 5:4). When we're dishonest with other people, do we think about the fact that we're also being dishonest with God?

Ananias and Saphira were caught up in appearing to be generous to the church. They were creating a persona of kindness and generosity, not knowing that the Holy Spirit would expose them and they would lose their lives. How many times have we lost friends and destroyed relationships because we couldn't be honest? We hid behind a mask that made us appear open and honest, but we weren't. Usually, people find out about our true colors, and then we are exposed for who we really are.

While the couple did sell some of their possessions and did offer part of the proceeds, they weren't completely honest. You could call what they did a half-truth; but often a half-truth becomes a whole lie. When we hold back parts of the truth, our actions destroy the trust others have in us. They don't know if they can fully trust us again.

When Ananias and Saphira lied, they lost their lives. This shows us that the danger of lying is that something always dies. Whether it's trust, love, communication, respect, faithfulness, the entire relationship—dishonesty brings about death. Every time we lie, we kill our relationships little by little.

BASED ON the counseling I do with married couples, I'd say that around 90 percent of them who have experienced infidelity say that they couldn't talk to their spouses. That lack of communication masks what's going on in the relationship and it keeps each person from being honest. So instead of talking to their spouses, they go to work, to church, or to the gym and find someone else to talk to.

What starts out as innocent conversations and "venting" become deep emotional attachments. Before long, that person is sharing his or her heart with someone other than the person he or she married. And as the Bible says, "For where your treasure is, there will your heart be also" (Matthew 6:21).

THE SUCCESS of our relationships is not predicated on physical attraction or by how many material possessions we own. It's not about what car you drive or the neighborhood you live in. Instead, relationship success is built on the foundation of trust and honesty. If you can't be honest, your foundation is already weak.

First Timothy 4:2 relates lying with having a seared conscience. The more a person lies, the easier he or she will find it to lie. After a while, that person won't mind lying about anything, even when he or she doesn't have to. And that person will also not be able to distinguish between a truth and a lie. It will all be the same.

If you're struggling with being honest, consider the following:

In general, how honest are you? Take an assessment of how honest you are, even outside your relationship. Do you lie at work? Do you automatically lie to avoid getting in trouble? Do you lie to your friends and family members? Do you lie to God? Why do you lie? Is lying easy for you? If you are lying to everyone, even when you don't have to, and lying has become a way of life for you, seek spiritual counseling. You might have deeper issues that need to be dealt with. Until you deal with lying, you won't be able to be completely honest in marriage.

Work on being honest in everything you say or do. Make a commitment to be honest, even when it's difficult and you fear the outcome. Talk with your spouse about your desire to be honest and your struggles to do so. Don't be afraid to go with your spouse to talk with a marital or spiritual counselor.

Seek God for help. God abhors lying. He wants us to be honest in all of our transactions and relationships, not just marriage. But honesty and trust in marriage go hand in hand, so it's key to a successful relationship. But if lying has become a way of life, along with professional help, ask God for strength and courage to be honest.

Reflect

Ask yourself the following questions. Answer as honestly and thoughtfully as you can. Reflect on your answers, and use them to help you learn how to be more honest.

1. Do I struggle with being honest? Why?

2. Am I as honest with others as I would like them to be honest with me?

3. In relationships, do I hold back part of the truth? Do I find it difficult to be completely honest with others?

4. In what ways has dishonesty (my own or others') hurt me?

5. How can I become more honest and open in communicating with others?

– Chapter 9 –

Ministry

"[A bishop is] one that ruleth well his own house . . . for if a man know not how to rule his own house, how shall he take care of the church of God?" 1 Timothy 3:4-5

Ministry is an all-encompassing aspect of Kingdom work, and it's not just limited to those who are ordained to stand in the pulpit. The apostle Paul said, "When he ascended up on high, he led captivity captive, and gave gifts unto men," which means Jesus gave gifts to all of mankind, so everyone has a ministry.

Ministry has a broader context. It's not just what you do in church, but it's the life you live every day, including marriage.

By definition, ministry is about serving others, so the ministry of marriage involves husbands and wives ministering to each other through love, support, security, and trust. But that ministry isn't only about what couples do for each other. It also involves what they model to the world. Through marriage, couples unfold a mystery and show a picture of Christ's love for the church.

PRISCILLA AND Aquila are a good example of a biblical couple who ministered to and with each other. "Harmoniously, they labored together in the service of the church." The couple, living in Corinth, were "honored and much-loved friends of Paul" as he made his missionary journeys, so much so, that he stayed with them for 18 months. The husband and wife team were true friends who "laid down their own necks" to save Paul (Romans 16:4). "They walked as one because they had unanimously agreed to put Christ first." They were so united, that in all of the references to them in the Bible, they are always named together. Not only did they share their Christian ministry, but they also worked together, with Paul, as tentmakers, so they spent an incredible amount of time together.

God also used this couple to lead Apollos, a fiery preacher with limited knowledge, to a greater understanding of salvation through the cross. They were so helpful to him that "he became so mighty in the Gospel that he was called an apostle!"[1]

WHEN JESUS gave His final instructions to His disciples before He ascended, He said, "But ye shall receive power, after that the Holy Ghost is come upon you, and ye shall be witnesses unto me both in Jerusalem, and in all Judaea, and in Samaria, and unto the uttermost part of the earth" (Acts 1:8). That verse says so much, but for our purposes, let's look at two things.

First, God, through the Holy Spirit, has given us great power to do what He has commanded us to do. He has not left us to figure things out on our own nor given us such great tasks that we have to depend on our own power to do them. Let's face it. There are just some things that we can't do without the supernatural power of the Holy Spirit.

When two people get married, it's essential for them to invite God into their relationship. Not only does God's presence in their marriage provide a solid foundation for them to build on, but the Holy Spirit becomes the engine to power their relationship. Ephesians 5:18 says, "And be not drunk with wine, wherein is excess; but be filled with the Spirit." Our Creator God knows that in our flesh there are things we don't have the power to do. It's not in our nature to be monogamous, faithful, and submitted. God offers His Spirit to empower us to successfully minister in our marriages, which is why we have to be full of the Spirit so we can possess the power God wants us to have.

Then Jesus gave His disciples a map to best carry out their assignment. He told them they would be witnesses in "Jerusalem, . . . all Judaea, . . . in Samaria, and unto the uttermost part of the earth"—in that order. Why is the order of those places so important? It's not the specific places necessarily that are important, but it's their locations.

Jesus mentioned Jerusalem first because it was where they were currently located. In other words, they were to start their ministries in their hometown, at home. Only when they had ministered in Jerusalem could they then branch out and go to "all Judaea," which expanded their reach to the surrounding region. Then they were to go to Samaria, a lot farther away. And only then should they minister to "the uttermost part of the earth." Jesus was teaching an important lesson about ministering where you are first and then reaching out beyond your immediate area.

Sometimes people find it extremely easy to minister to everyone but to their spouses. On any given day of the week, you can find them helping the homeless, feeding the hungry, or volunteering to work more hours at the office.

They will eagerly take in someone else's child or spend hours at the church cleaning up. But what have they done at home? How have they ministered to their husbands or wives? Why build houses for Habitat for Humanity when your own house is falling down?

As the saying goes, "Charity begins at home." It's not selfish to start your ministry at home and serve your spouse before venturing out farther from home. Flight attendants tell you that in the event of an emergency, you should secure your own oxygen mask before trying to help others secure theirs. If you're not ministering at home first, how can you minister to someone in your neighborhood, at church, at work, at school, or across the country?

YEARS AGO, I was invited to speak at a marriage conference in Fort Wayne, Indiana. It was the first time I had been asked to speak at such a conference. My wife and I had been married for about seven years at that time, and she went with me. After I spoke, many of the attendees were saying how gifted I was and how much they enjoyed my session. That made me feel great!

During the question-and-answer period, my wife raised her hand and asked a question. I didn't think much of it. I answered her question and moved on to the next person.

I didn't really know Bishop T. D. Jakes back then, but what he said to me changed my life. He saw that my wife had asked me a question, and later he pulled me aside and asked, "Why is your wife asking questions at your session?" I didn't know what to tell him. I guessed that she just wanted to know the answer. He then told me that her asking me questions at the conference showed my lack of ministry at home. He said it was a commentary on me as a preacher and a pastor and that anything that I'm getting ready to preach or teach in public should have already been shared with my wife at home. Not doing that made me a hypocrite.

That was hard to hear, but I knew there was truth in what Bishop Jakes said. In 1 Timothy 3:4-5, Paul tells Timothy the qualifications for the office of a bishop, or one who ministers. A bishop is "one that ruleth well his own house . . . for if a man know not how to rule his own house, how shall he take care of the church of God?" From that time on, I followed his wise counsel and began to minister to my wife at home first.

I have a young couple in my church who are active in the community, but the wife took the first step. She's a teacher and works at the local youth center. Her husband is a police officer, but he wasn't involved in her ministry in the beginning.

To get him involved, she asked him to accompany her to the youth center. She told him she would feel safer with him around. He went initially for that reason; but once he started going regularly, he saw a need to mentor some of the young boys who gathered there. There are all kinds of ways to open up your ministry to your spouse and share it with them and get them involved.

I've always been inspired by Pastors Creflo and Taffy Dollar. They are a great example of a husband and wife who are successful ministers. Each of them knows where they flourish best. Pastor Creflo isn't trying to be Pastor Taffy, and Pastor Taffy isn't trying to be Pastor Creflo. They complement each other, and their ministry is like a seamless thread—you can't tell where one begins and the other ends. Each of them can do different things, and they fill in the gaps for each other as needed. So when they come together, they are greater than the sum of their parts.

TO HELP you to better understand ministry in relationships, consider the following:

Minister to your spouse first. Jesus was clear about us beginning our ministries where we are. Don't be so quick to minister to your city or state or the world. Before you take on ministering to others, begin at home by serving your spouse. You can't neglect your spouse but be loving, kind, helpful, and generous to everyone else.

When people see the discrepancy between how you serve and minister to your spouse and how you serve and minister to those outside your home, it will be hard for them to hear anything you're saying. Show God's love and care to your spouse first before you minister to others.

Share your ministry with your spouse. Once you've learned how to minister to your spouse, share your ministry with your spouse. If you're doing something away from home (such as volunteering, preaching, teaching, serving), first, share it with your spouse. Show him or her what's in your heart, and talk with your spouse about what God has given you. Share with him or her what you'd like to say to a broader audience, and consider asking your spouse to join you in that assignment.

Reflect

Ask yourself the following questions, and answer as honestly and thoughtfully as you can. Then use your responses as a way to prepare yourself for ministry in and through marriage.

1. What type of ministry do I have? What type of ministry will I have with my spouse?

2. How has my marriage become a ministry?

3. How can I improve the ministry of my marriage?

4. What marriages have I seen that modeled effective ministry?

5. Does my ministry bring glory to God? How?

— Chapter 10 —

Love

"Walk in love, as Christ also hath loved us, and hath given himself for us an offering and a sacrifice to God." (Ephesians 5:2)

People who are looking forward to getting married may take for granted that love is just part of the whole package. But where does love come from? How can we love another person the way we should? The answer comes in God's Word.

First John 4:8 says succinctly and to the point, "God is love." We could stop right there. That phrase answers the questions, Where did love come from? What should love look like? We don't have to look any further than God because He is love. He is the source of love.

But John continues: "In this was manifested the love of God toward us, because that God sent his only begotten Son into the world, that we might live through him. Herein is love, not that we loved God, but that he loved us, and sent his Son to be the propitiation for our sins" (1 John 4:9-10).

In this passage, John shows us love and sacrifice, two key parts of marriage. God loved us so much that He gave up something of incredible value—His Son, Jesus—to show us His love. But more importantly, God didn't love us because we loved Him first. Instead, He loved us before we ever loved Him. So God's love wasn't dependent on anything we had done for Him or because we showed Him love. This establishes the pattern that Christ models through His love for His bride, the church.

We have to be loved by God before we can love others, and He gives us the perfect example. He shows us that love is not selfish, and it's not always easy. Sometimes it will require that we make sacrifices. But if we include God in our attempts to love, we won't have to go it alone.

That's because when we place God in His rightful place, He becomes the foundation for marriage and helps us do what we can't do alone. Ecclesiastes 4:12 says, "A threefold cord is not quickly broken." So marriage doesn't have to be the husband and the wife struggling to figure out what love is and trying desperately to love each other. The third strand of that cord is Christ. He strengthens us to do great things in and through marriage, and He sustains our relationships.

IN ORDER to experience love, we have to go to the Source. Many people are frantically searching for love in all the wrong places because they don't know God, who is love. When we are in relationship with God, we are experiencing true love. He is our Creator, and He loved us so much that He gave His Son, Jesus. There is no greater love than that. God's love is not selfish, and often it's not even reciprocated. His love isn't conditional on anything we do. It just is.

Matthew wrote about an encounter Jesus had with one of the Pharisees. The Pharisee asked, "Master, which is the great commandment of the law?" Jesus responded, "Thou shalt love the Lord thy God with all thy heart, and with all thy soul, and with all thy mind. This is the first and great commandment. And the second is like unto it, Thou shalt love thy neighbor as thyself" (Matthew 22:36-39).

So Jesus is giving us a practical equation for being able to love. First, we should love God with everything we have. Then we're to love others as we love ourselves. If we're not already in relationship with God, then we're going to find it difficult to receive love. And if we don't love ourselves, we won't be able to love others.

WHEN WE read in Genesis that God said it's not good for Adam to be alone, we assume that Eve is about to appear. But that's not what happens. God spent a considerable amount of time with Adam before He gave him companionship. God also presented the animals to Adam so that Adam might name them. Only after God established a relationship with Adam and gave him several assignments did He then create Eve.

At that point, Adam was ready for his wife. We have to remember that our need doesn't negate our readiness. Just because we may need something doesn't mean we're ready for it. God wants us to know Him so that when He blesses us, we won't put anything in His place. He also wants us to know ourselves and love ourselves so that we can better love our neighbors. Then God provides us with vision. How can we lead someone else if we don't know where we're going? He also makes provisions for us so we have something to take care of and then offer in a relationship.

It's easy to grow impatient with the Creation story because we're anxious for Eve to make her appearance. But God is all-wise and all-knowing. His delay in presenting

Eve to Adam was all part of God's plan. In our lives, God knows what we need, but He also knows what we need to do before our needs are met.

Plenty of people rush into marriage because they believe that they need a husband or a wife immediately. But how many people have slowed down and taken the time to ask God what they need first? Probably not very many. They're anxious and impatient and want a spouse now. But God may be preparing them in a way that they're not aware of. They also may be ignoring God's timing and following their own. That's not a good idea.

God created us, and He knows that we desire to love and be loved. But we need to trust Him that His plan for us is better than our own plan. Trust God for love, and rest in His faithfulness as you wait.

SOME COUPLES include the reading of 1 Corinthians 13 in their wedding ceremonies because it talks about love. But I often wonder if they have actually read it and understand what love will require from them.

Paul says, "Love suffereth long, and is kind; love envieth not; love vaunteth not itself, is not puffed up, doth not behave itself unseemly, seeketh not its own, is not provoked, taketh not account of evil; rejoiceth not in unrighteousness, but rejoiceth with the truth; beareth all things, believeth all things, hopeth all things, endureth all things. Love never faileth" (1 Corinthians 13:4-8, American Standard Version).

After reading how Paul has defined and outlined love, it's a wonder anyone gets married! That's an incredibly high standard to meet. But it shows us that love is not fleeting like lust and infatuation, which disguise themselves as love. Love is not selfish or based on temporal things such as physical attraction or money. Love doesn't disappear because a spouse gets sick or loses a job. Instead, it "suffereth long, and is kind. . . . Love never faileth" (1 Corinthians 13:4, 8).

We might think Paul's definition of *love* is unattainable, but it's important that we strive for it daily because we serve as vessels of God's amazing love. I've known people who have taken in children and raised them as their own. I knew a woman who worked two jobs so her husband could finish law school. We live among great examples of people loving others and putting the needs of others before their own, so it's not impossible to reach for that high standard of love.

I talked with a minister who said something that encapsulates what love in marriage is. I was visiting City of Refuge, a church in Los Angeles, and I met one of the ministers on staff. He told me that his wife had kidney disease and that she needed a kidney. I couldn't imagine how devastating an experience that was for him and his wife. I told him I would pray for her. But he kindly told me that I didn't need to pray because he was going to give her one of his kidneys.

I was astounded. I reminded him that once he gave away his kidney, it wouldn't grow back. Of course, he knew that, but he wasn't to be deterred. In fact, he was insistent. He loved his wife so much that he was willing to give her part of his body so that she could live. That's one of the greatest expressions of love I've ever known!

AS PAUL said, love "suffereth long." In other words, love is patient. Some spouses grow impatient rather quickly. Some will seek divorce because they have already thrown in the towel and given up. But Paul encourages us to let love temper us and help us to be patient with those we love. None of is perfect, and for some of us, it takes a little longer to get where we need to go.

A woman in my church would ask me to pray for her husband every Sunday. As soon as I finished preaching in the first service and was on my way to my second service, she'd be there waiting for me.

"We gotta pray!" she'd say.

"What are we praying for this week?" I'd ask, trying to hurry her along so I could prepare for the next service.

"We gotta pray that my husband gets saved." It didn't matter that we had prayed the same prayer the week before and the week before that.

"So what did he do this time?"

"He came home drunk."

So, once again, we'd pray for her husband to be saved. I had begun to think my prayers weren't working and that she would come to believe I was a false prophet because her husband didn't seem any closer to getting saved now than when we first started praying. But we prayed for her husband for ten years; and every Sunday, the prayer was the same—that he would be saved.

One Sunday, after the first service, I didn't see her. I knew I needed to move on to the second service and I could only wait a few more minutes. Then she came up to me, crying. I thought, *This can't be good*. I asked her what happened.

"Do you remember when all those people went up to the altar and got saved this morning? Well, my husband was one of them!"

I was thrilled! Her husband had finally gotten saved! I puffed out my chest a bit because I couldn't help but feel somewhat responsible for this miracle. Not only had I been praying for this man for ten years, but I thought I had preached one of my best sermons that morning.

"Well, I'm glad I was on it this morning!" I bragged. But then her husband appeared and burst my ego.

"I'm sorry, Pastor. I don't want to hurt your ego, but it wasn't your sermon that did it."

"Then what was it?"

"Many nights, I came home drunk. Sometimes, I'd even bring my friends home after we'd been drinking, shooting pool, and partying. My wife would get out of bed and fix dinner for us. My friends were amazed at how kind she was, and they would ask me why she was so nice to us, especially after we had arrived at the house drunk. I told them she was like that because she loves God and she loves me. They told me I was crazy to hang out all night with them when I had such a wonderful wife waiting for me at home.

"From that day on, I wanted to get to know this God my wife was always talking about. I wondered how God could give her such strength and love to put up with all of my mess. How could she fix dinner for me and my drunken friends without getting angry? That's what made me want to get to know Jesus as personal Savior, because she showed me so much love and wasn't getting anything from me in return."

Sometimes when we love, it will be difficult because we may think that we're not getting love in return. Or we may become frustrated because the person we love isn't responding in the way we think they should. But Paul reminds us that love is patient, kind, and it endures. Even when we get tired and we're ready to give up, love continues. More importantly, we are God's representatives of love in this world. If we don't love as we should, how will people see the love of Christ?

HOW CHRIST loves the church is the pattern for marriage. So how are you modeling Christ for your spouse?

One day, my wife told me that she was having a problem with God. I was puzzled. Who has a problem with God? I told her that she had to be a backslider. But what she said next shocked me.

"I'm having a problem with God because of you. If you're representing Him, and this is how God is, then I don't know if I can trust Him."

That hit me like a ton of bricks. I had no idea I was painting such a bad picture of God to my wife, or to anyone. I knew I had to change. I had to do a better job of being God's representative.

If you're not modeling God's love, what do people see in you?

WHEN ASKED, most people will say that the opposite of love is hate. But that's not what the Bible says. First John 4:18 says, "There is no fear in love; but perfect love casteth out fear: because fear hath torment. He that feareth is not made perfect in love." So the opposite of love is fear.

When we know that God loves us, we don't have to fear anything. The psalmist said, "Yea, though I walk through the valley of the shadow of death, I will fear no evil: for thou art with me" (Psalm 23:4). People live in fear because they don't trust God or believe that He's with them.

It's this fear that corrupts a couple's marriage, and it erodes their trust in each other. It is this fear that drives a wife to check her husband's phone to see who he's calling and texting, a husband to hack his wife's social media accounts, a wife to search her husband's pockets for signs of infidelity, or a husband to spy on his wife at the grocery store. Where is the love? In the absence of love there is fear. Our fear creates insecurities and hurt feelings, which fester and poison our relationships.

But if we have God in our marriages, we shouldn't have a reason to fear. Having God as an integral part of our relationship should foster love and leave no room for fear.

IN PREPARING yourself to love, consider the following:

Look to God for love. God is love, so He is the source of love. Reflect on your relationship with Him and God's love for you. Then think about Christ's love for the church as a pattern of self-giving love. Read passages of Scripture that will remind you of this amazing love, and use those as your roadmap for showing love for others.

Learn to love yourself. Jesus said that after loving God, we are to love others as we love ourselves. But it's difficult to love others in that way if we've never learned to love ourselves. If you need counseling to help you learn to love yourself, don't be afraid or ashamed to reach out for help.

Invite God into your relationship. When God is the foundation of a relationship, you can be confident that He'll strengthen you to do what you can't do on your own and that He will sustain your relationship. Ask Him to be part of that threefold cord (Ecclesiastes 4:12) and to be an integral, foundational part of your relationship.

Reflect

Ask yourself the following questions, and answer as honestly and thoughtfully as you can. Then use your responses as a way to prepare yourself to give and to receive love in marriage.

1. What is my definition of *love*? Am I ready for love?

2. How does loving Christ and having a relationship with Him relate to loving a spouse and building a successful marriage? Does my love resemble God's love, or does my love more resemble the world's interpretation of love?

3. How does loving myself help me to better love others?

4. Are there any aspects of love that I struggle with? Which ones? How can I overcome my struggles with love?

5. What is my response to 1 Corinthians 13? Does the love I have reflect what Paul outlines in that chapter?

NOTES

CHAPTER 1

[1-4]Focus on the Family (focusonthefamily.com/marriage/promos/healthy -marriage-traits/managing-shared-responsibility).

CHAPTER 3

[1]From *Baker's Evangelical Dictionary* (biblestudytools.com/dictionaries /bakers-evangelical-dictionary/kinsman-redeemer.html).

CHAPTER 4

[1]From "All the Women of the Bible—Gomer," Biblegateway (bible gateway.com/resources/all-women-bible/Gomer).

CHAPTER 5

[1]From "The Power of Vision for Your Marriage," by Jimmy Evans, Marriage Today (marriagetoday.com/marriagehelp/the-power-of-vision -for-marriage/).

CHAPTER 9

[1]From "All the Women of the Bible—Priscilla," Biblegateway (https:// www.biblegateway.com/resources/all-women-bible/Priscilla).

www.ingramcontent.com/pod-product-compliance
Lightning Source LLC
Chambersburg PA
CBHW020619120726
47905CB00003B/857